# black
# boxes

Other books written by Caroline Smailes

*In Search of Adam*
*Disraeli Avenue*

# Caroline Smailes

# Black Boxes

FRIDAY
FICTION

The Friday Project
An imprint of HarperCollins Publishers
77–85 Fulham Palace Road, Hammersmith, London W6 8JB

www.thefridayproject.co.uk
www.harpercollins.co.uk

First published by The Friday Project in 2008
This paperback edition published by The Friday Project in 2009
Copyright © Caroline Smailes 2008

1

Caroline Smailes asserts the moral right to
be identified as the author of this work

A catalogue record for this book is available from the British Library

ISBN 978-1-90-632190-1

Typeset by Wordsense Ltd, Edinburgh (www.wordsense co.uk)

Printed and bound in Great Britain by Clays Ltd, St Ives plc

**Mixed Sources**
Product group from well-managed
forests and other controlled sources
www.fsc.org  Cert no. SW-COC-1806
© 1996 Forest Stewardship Council

FSC is a non-profit international organisation established to promote the
responsible management of the world's forests. Products carrying the FSC
label are independently certified to assure consumers that they come
from forests that are managed to meet the social, economic and
ecological needs of present or future generations.

Find out more about HarperCollins and the environment at
**www.harpercollins.co.uk/green**

A Promise.

For my son. *Jacob*.

For my son. *Benjamin*.

For my daughter. *Poppy Elisabeth*.

'Aha!' she cried mockingly, 'you would fetch your dearest, but the beautiful bird sits no longer singing in the nest; the cat has got it, and will scratch out your eyes as well. Rapunzel is lost to you; you will never see her again.'

**_Rapunzel_ – Jacob and Wilhelm Grimm**

'The man had not known one happy hour since he had left the children in the forest; the woman, however, was dead. Gretel emptied her pinafore until pearls and precious stones ran about the room, and Hansel threw one handful after another out of his pocket to add to them. Then all anxiety was at an end, and they lived together in perfect happiness.'

**_Hansel and Gretel_ – Jacob and Wilhelm Grimm**

From _The Project Gutenberg Etext Fairy Tales_, by the Grimm Brothers, April, 2001 [Etext #2591]

# Context

## 1. Black Box (*noun*)

a. An informal term for an event-recording device, most commonly associated with aircraft. It is recovered after a crash and its contents examined for clues as to why the crash occurred.

b. An informal term for an event-recording device, used creatively to give voice to Ana Lewis. It has been recovered after the crash of Ana Lewis' life and its contents are being examined for clues to help determine why the crash of Ana Lewis occurred.

## 2. Crash (*noun*)

a. A collision of moving vehicles, often caused by a catastrophic sequence of events and leading to a total breakdown in ability to function.

b. A collision of Ana Lewis and Alexander Edwards, caused by a catastrophic sequence of events and leading to Ana's total breakdown in ability to function.

# BLACK
# BOX #01

Flight Recorder
**DO NOT OPEN**

---

**[55°01'01.54" N 1°27'28.83" W]**

Bedroom. Ana's first floor flat in a Victorian house near the coast of Tynemouth. The room contains a wardrobe, a bed and a bedside table. The walls are red. The duvet cover is red. On the bedside table there is an empty glass and an open pair of scissors. Next to the empty glass there are two white rectangular boxes. One of them once contained sleeping tablets. The other once contained painkillers.

---

*~Are you still there?~*
You've ruined the end.
Now I know what's going to happen.
The plot has you coming back to kill me.
A twist in the narrative.

[five second silence]

I had cast you in the role of handsome prince.
How strange that you should turn out to be my killer.
But that's an end.
And now I need to find a beginning.

---

*~Are you there?~*
*~Will you listen?~*
*~Do you remember?~*
I am remembering when we were courting.
It was always cold.
I'm thinking back to when you wrapped your arm
around me as we walked along Tynemouth beach.
I remember you folding me into you.
The image is practically cinematic.
*~Do you remember?~*

[five second silence]

We wore matching scarves.
I had knitted them and they had holes where I had
dropped stitches.

You had laughed at my fumbling attempt.

[sound: a throaty laugh]

I had dropped many stitches.

But you said that you loved them.

*~Didn't you?~*

That they were perfectly us.

*~Do you remember?~*

The scarves wrapped around us.

They bound us together.

You could climb up your scarf to mine.

*~Do you remember?~*

And then you found that knobbly washed-up stick.

And you wrote our names in the sand in those huge
perfectly straight lines.

And those lines stood together and made the
flawlessly straight letters of our names.

ALEX+ANA.

You said that our names and our lives and
everything that we would ever choose to do would
be straight.

And I thought that you liked that.

[sound: sniff sniff]

I thought that the neatness and the organisation and
the perfectly horizontalness.

Well I thought that you liked that.

[volume: ↑ high]

No kinks and no bends.
A perfectly straight route from here to there.
From there to here.
To nowhere else.
And on that day when you wrote our two names
into the sand.
Well I didn't realise that one day.
When you wanted.
That you'd wash away the +ANA that was joined to
the ALEX.

[sound: sobbing]

[silence]

But your name would never go away.
It grew fainter, but it is still there.
I still see it there.
I can still see ALEX+ANA.

[sound: throat clearing]

You started a new life.
ALEX+SUE.
But I can't write another name.
There are no other names that are perfectly straight
and perfectly able to cover ALEX.

[silence]

But you went off.
And you found that new name.
And it had curves in it because you had decided that

you preferred curves.
The lines no longer needed to be straight.
You adapted.
You accepted.
You left me here.
You left me.
Trapped.

[silence]

---

My room is a box.
A black box.
A sometimes ruby red box.
     *~Is that confusing?~*
You trapped me in here.

[voiced: unrecognisable word]

[volume: low]

I have a front.
I have a back.
They are my window and my door.
My door takes me to my children.
My door keeps me from your Pip and my Davie.
Our two children.
     *~They are your children too.~*
     *~But you know that they are your children
      too!~*

*~Am I trying to be too clever?~*

The view from my window is ever changing.

I see the sand.

I see the sea.

And that image is my painting mounted in a chipped red window frame.

A sometimes black window frame.

A perfect square.

A perfect painting.

A painting that holds the memories of you and me.

---

We met as students.

*~I know that you remember that.~*

We lived in the same halls.

On the same corridor.

And we met in the first week.

You were so quiet.

All the girls wanted to know you.

To know what made you tick.

You were different.

You carried books around with you.

And you read those books.

You had a guitar.

And you could play your guitar.

Your friends were all girls.

You preferred female company.
And although girls flashed their breasts at you and
although girls flicked their flowing hair and offered
themselves to you.
You never accepted.
You had integrity.
It covered you in a bubble.
It protected you.

> *~When did it pop?~*
> *~When did the bubble burst?~*
> *~Was it when you selected that girl from that*
>   *magazine and trimmed her flawless edge?~*

I love(*d*) you.
I used to watch you playing your guitar in the
common room.
And I love(*d*) you.

> *~Did you realise then?~*

We were friends before we were anything else.
We were friends that became something else.

[silence]

But not until our second year
I was chair of the Poetry Society.
You'd come along to listen.

> *~Did you realise that they were all about*
>   *you?~*

You used to listen.

You never clapped.

And then afterwards you'd always want to walk me home.

Sometimes you'd hold my hand.

And we'd walk in silence.

Words didn't carry meaning for you.

> *~How many hours did we spend together?~*
> *~How many hours passed in silence?~*

And I always preferred your place to mine.

You lived alone.

You preferred it that way.

You liked your own space.

One room – bedroom/lounge/kitchen.

And then a door to your grubby toilet.

Your furniture was shabby.

Your toilet was always grubby.

> *~No it was filthy!~*

But in the corner, just beside the sunken brown armchair.

Your guitar rested against the wall.

But the guitar would wait, as you mixed, rolled and twisted the end of your joint.

Then you'd balance the smooth roll of paper onto your lip and you'd strum.

And you'd sing your sad sad songs.

And the lyrics wouldn't connect with me and

with us.

They were of places and experiences that we'd never shared.

But I wanted to recognise myself within your words.

I wanted to hear you recount experiences that we'd shared.

To be singing about a depth of emotion that you had suffered because of me.

And that's why I kept coming back.

*~You didn't realise did you?~*

I wanted to make you feel something in the hope that you would commemorate me in your words.

Like you had for the Indian Girl.

That you would give me a purpose in being.

Because you stirred me when you sang and you strummed.

You turned something on within me.

You made me want the performer in you.

And I'd wish that you'd sing and strum something that would make my insides explode.

A song to communicate the words that you never spoke to me.

[sound: humming of an unrecognisable tune]

That was before we ever kissed.

I used to think that first kiss was an afterthought.

A something that you never really meant to happen.

That we'd travelled as far as our friendship could go.
And that the only possible next step was a kiss.
A kiss that should never have been.

[five second silence]

But it did.
And we did.
And then Pip did.
And once when I questioned why you sang
such sad sad songs about places and times and
happenings that I never understood.
You said, **I sing them because I like them**.
And that, **the words don't matter**.
That, **it's about the way things join together**.
**How they loop.**
**How the syllables become beats.**
**How the beats have to fit.**
It was a timing thing with you.
It was a red thing with me.
The view from here is red.

[sound: humming of same now vaguely recognisable tune]

---

I had short hair when we met.
*~Do you remember?~*
I spiked it with cheap gel.
That was then.

Now my hair grows long.
If you call out at my window, I will let my hair fall
down to you.

---

I must remember to *blink*.
My eyes are dry as I stare out of my window.
Red eyes.
I want to dip my fingernails into my eyes and I want
to scratch and scratch and scratch my itch.
But I don't.
But I can't.

[sound: fingertips tapping surface]

A memory may flake off and stick under my nail.
And I won't be able to put it back into my eye.
And then I will forget.
And I can't let that happen.
My memories are all that I have.

[sound: sobbing]

So I look out of my window.

[ten second silence]

And I look onto the sand and I don't *blink*.
And if I stare and stare and stare through the pain.
Then I can see our names.
I see.
ALEX+ANA.

Then I lie flat.

[sound: a body flopping back onto bed]

My back stuck to my red duvet.

My arms and legs a perfectly straight X.

I open myself.

I open all of myself.

Waiting for you to re-enter into my picture.

I know that you'll return.

>*~Are you there?~*
>
>*~Can you hear me?~*

You're waiting for me to die.

>*~Are you there?~*

You're waiting to see if you've killed me.

[silence]

I am trapped.

I will not leave this black square box.

[sound: pinging of a filament in a light bulb]

---

When we were students you liked to sing.

I liked to sing too.

You once told me that I had a sweet voice.

>*~Did you once say that?~*

I'm not too sure that you did.

I remember one day.

I couldn't tolerate hearing the same sad song over

and over.

About the same Indian Girl.

And how she had broken your heart.

So I asked you why you didn't write a new song.

Something about the two of us.

We'd been together for over a year.

>*~And do you remember what you said to*
>    *me?~*

You said, **I can't write about you**.

You laughed when you said that.

And you said, **the Indian Girl is the only girl that I have
ever loved**.

That, **nothing could compare to her**.

I never asked her name.

>*~Would you even have told me?~*

[sound: glass smashing]

---

[two second silence]

From the beginning we had problems.

Sexual.

>*~I know that the topic makes you*
>    *uncomfortable, but I want to talk about it.~*

I have to talk about this now.

There won't be another time.

*~You've seen to that haven't you?~*
We've never spoken about our sexual problems.
*~Where to begin?~*
You had a problem entering me.
With intimacy.
From the very beginning.

[sound: a loud sigh]

*~Yes you did.~*
Your erections were laughable.
And the story of our passion failed to have a
beginning, middle and end.
*~Do you understand what I mean by this?~*
*~I don't think that you do!~*
You weren't erect or you were erect.
Nothing in between.
And it seemed to me that the level of your stiffness
had nothing to do with me.
I wasn't involved.
It was an up and down kind of thing.
There was nothing that I could do.
And I tried.
I tried everything.
Everything.
I feel embarrassed.

[voiced: unrecognisable words]

[volume: low]

At what I allowed you to do to me.
> *~Do you even know that I tried?~*

---

You'd blame the drugs.
You'd praise the drugs.
> *~Do you remember?~*

I know that you're clean now.
That all stopped when I was pregnant.
Everything stopped when I was pregnant.
> *~But do you remember sex and your joints?~*
> *~Do you remember the potion that they
>   created together?~*

The sparks that you lit.
> *~Do you remember how you could go on and
>   on and on?~*

And that there would be no middle.
And that there would be no end.
You would just stop.
Out of exhaustion.
> *~Or was it boredom?~*

But for me it was pain.
> *~I've never told you this before.~*

You see.
You never considered that you were hurting me.
That your constant pounding.

That your sweat-dripping performance hurt me
inside.

You see.

I was too dry.

    *~Yes dry.~*

                        [sound: cackle of laughter]

In all of the waiting and hoping for an erection and
in all of the needing to instantly react the moment
stiffness emerged.

Well there was no thought for me.

You didn't consider that I needed to be turned on.

That I needed my buttons to be flicked.

So you made my insides red.

And I longed for the end.

I longed for the fucking to finish.

And I would fake.

    *~You didn't realise that I faked?~*

You thought that you were a God.

My moans and arched back were perfectly timed.

I told a story.

I made it all up.

You see.

You weren't a God.

Not in bed.

Not in our bed.

    *~Do you realise that you were really crap in*

*bed?~*
*~Has Sue ever mentioned it to you?~*
*~Does she fake?~*
*~Are you sure that you could tell?~*

You see.

A performance can be too perfect.

I used to wait for the applause.

[sound: sharp clap clap clap]

You should ask Sue if she fakes.

---

You were the worst of my eighteen.

Congratulations.

I've made you a certificate.

It's hanging in a shell-covered frame.

If I open my eyes.

And if I stare out from my black box, then I can see your framed certificate.

Suspended in the air.

Just above where the tide meets the shore.

[sound: thumping scrape of window frame on wood]

[silence]

---

*~Do you know that I pleasure myself?~*
It was a skill that I learned during our time together.

I'd work myself until the tips of my fingers became numb.
I used to think about you when I did it.
I don't now.
Not always.

[silence]

---

*Noun:* Masturbation.
The encouragement of one's own genitals.
*Etymology:* Latin origin.
Perhaps.
Manus being 'hand', and turbare to excite or stir up.
It entered English in the eighteenth century.
Possibly.
It's a nice word.
A nice strong stimulating word.

[sound: a guttural laugh]

---

Red and white make pink.
The view is not pink.
The view from here is red.
*Blink.*
*Blink.*

[silence]

I can count on my right hand the number of times
that I have seen your sperm.
Your spunk.
Your come.
I have never tasted it.

~*Has Sue?*~

[sound: a guttural laugh]

---

~*Do you remember when I asked you if you
love(d) me?*~
We'd been together for about two years.
And I love(*d*) you.
I'd always love(*d*) you.
And I told you.
Over and over.
Sometimes I was overwhelmed with love for you
and the words would burst out.

[voiced: [b] sound]

[volume: high]

Voiced bilabial plosive.
I used to be clever.

[voiced: [b] sound]

[volume: high]

Sometimes I was overwhelmed with love for you
and the words would burst out.

[voiced: I love you]

[volume: high]

Without restraint.

Highly stressed syllables would gush out without warning.

And I'd hate myself every time that I told you.

Because the silence that came after my words.

The silence that floated from your lips.

It was heavy.

It crashed to the floor and echoed around the room.

And then one day.

Fuelled with vodka and lime.

I asked you if you love(*d*) me.

*~And do you remember what you said?~*

*~Do you remember what you did?~*

You laughed.

[sound: a guttural ho ho ho laugh]

You told me, **I will never love you**.

You told me, **my heart is the size of a pea**.

That, **it is green and waiting to be mushy**.

I never asked you again.

I love(*d*) you.

---

It was about that time.

After you described your pea-sized heart.

That was the time when I stopped taking the
contraceptive pill.

    *~I know that I never told you.~*

    *~There didn't seem a point in telling you.~*

I stopped taking it because you never came inside
me.

You were never capable of coming inside me.

    *~And how could I talk to you about that?~*

I think that was the reason.

                                    [silence]

---

I have a favour to ask.

If you can hear me.

    *~Can you hear me?~*

It's for the next time that you come here.

And the time after that.

And the time after that.

    *~Can you bring me a strand of silk?~*

I read somewhere that it should be silk.

And I'm supposed to weave it all together and make
a ladder.

Perhaps it'd be easier if you just brought a ladder.

    *~Can you bring a really tall ladder?~*

We can use it to climb from my window when we
leave to live happily ever after.

[sound: a guttural laugh]

Some memories have holes in them.
Where I have *blink*ed too quickly.

[voiced: blink blink]

[volume: low]

> *~Oh please stop going on!~*
> *~I stopped taking the pill.~*
> *~And I never told you.~*
> *~It really isn't worth this fuss!~*

Everything was going fine between us.
It was fine.

> *~I wasn't trying to trap you.~*
> *~I know that's what you're thinking!~*
> *~But I wasn't.~*

At least I don't think that I was.
Holes.
I have white holes in the memories where my
eyelashes have ripped the surface.

[silence]

I really must stop *blink*ing.

[sound: humming, unrecognisable tune]

---

You didn't love me.

But I love(*d*) you.

It was simple.

Too simple.

I learned to live with it.

    *~No that's not true.~*

I live(*d*) in the hope that it would change.

That your pea-sized heart would expand.

And that it would become mushy because of me.

And that all of this would happen before it was too late.

That love for me would grow from your mushy heart.

That it would grow and grow.

Kind of like a leaf.

    *~Do peas have leaves?~*

I can't remember.

    [sound: undetectable objects thumping to the floor]

---

And then it happened.

    *~You know what I am talking about.~*

Perhaps you have forgotten the timing.

The placing.

The implications.

But you must remember.

It shocked us both.

I was in the second year of my PhD, studying the etymology of contemporary slang.

You were in the second year of your PhD in genetic engineering.

We'd been together for three years.

We both had paid teaching hours at the university.

We both had funding.

Money wasn't a problem.

We worked in different faculties.

We lived separately.

We saw each other a few times each week.

We had spare time.

I had days where I never spoke to you.

There was nothing wrong with our relationship.

We were plodding along.

[sound: distant rumbling of low flying aeroplane]

---

And then one day you came inside me.

[silence]

You ejaculated during sexual intercourse.

The words roll from my tongue.

It was quick.

You were quick.

~*Do you remember?*~

It shocked you.

It shocked me.

I asked you if it had happened.

I asked, *did you?*

And you nodded.

[sound: a laugh]

I could tell that you were shocked.

You couldn't find the words.

And I have never told you just how much your
sperm excited me.

I have thought about it so many times after that day.

I have thought about it when I was alone.

When I needed a release.

~*Yes I mean an orgasm!*~

~*Of course women need that kind of thing!*~

And that thought made a trail of discharge onto my
knickers.

I'd push my fingers down and over my soft hair.

I'd push my fingers inside me.

Until they were covered in my own juices.

And then that wetness made it easier for my fingers
to work their movements.

And then I'd rub my clitoris.

Caroline Smailes

To stimulate me.

Till I reached my climax.

And afterwards I would lick, suck and taste.

Hoping to experience your sperm.

[sound: sucking]

It's a natural thing.

Female masturbation.

It's a normal sexual act.

---

Sexual normality.

*~What is it to be sexually normal?~*

My lines are blurred.

I figure that normality would fall within the centre of your line.

*~Is that right?~*

And that the line should be Etchasketch straight.

*~Is that right?~*

*~But what is the scale from there to there?~*

*~And what acts must I pass through from there to there?~*

I don't have a ruler.

*~How can I pinpoint the exact centre?~*

I fear that my estimation may be slightly off.

*~Should I use my fingers?~*

26

[sound: unrecognisable sounds, possibly groans]

---

I had thirty-six hours.

I could have taken the morning-after pill.

I knew where to go and what to say.

The surgery on campus was always well stocked.

I could have gone.

Taken the pill.

Felt nauseous.

Probably thrown up.

And you'd never have known.

You'd probably not even have noticed.

But I didn't go.

I didn't think that there was a need.

I didn't think.

> *~I did think.~*

I didn't think.

> *~I did think.~*

I didn't think.

I don't know.

[sound: banging wardrobe door]

> *~Oh stop shouting!~*
>
> *~Stop the noise!~*

Your voice is too loud.

You're making me *blink*.

*Blink.*

*Blink.*

[sound: humming of an unrecognisable tune]

Your constant questioning is ruining my memory.

---

~*What do you mean?*~

I don't know what I was trying to achieve.

There wasn't a goal.

I dislike the word goal.

I'd be happier with aim.

Ambition.

Target.

Aspiration.

Goal carries connotations of sporting achievement.

Our intercourse was hardly award winning.

[sound: laugh to snort]

I didn't think.

Really I didn't.

[sound: laugh to snort]

---

I didn't think that there was a need.

I mean I remember knowing that I had thirty-six hours.

I remember thinking of hours.

And waiting for those hours to pass.
I could have taken the morning-after pill.
Perhaps I should have taken the morning-after pill.
   *~I didn't think.~*
I did think.
   *~I didn't think.~*
I did think.
   *~I didn't think.~*

---

I don't know.
I don't know.

[sound: distant rumbling of low flying aeroplane]

---

Ok. Ok.
   *~I did think!~*

[silence]

---

There was a moment.
It came like a wave.
I saw it coming.
And I began to think.
My mind began to wander into a future.
Into our future.
And I liked what I saw.

And so I rode.
I jumped in.
I allowed nature to decide.
It wasn't my decision.
~*It was out of my hands.*~
What would be would be.

[silence]

---

Que sera sera.

[sound: distant rumbling of low flying aeroplane]

---

~*Don't be angry.*~
~*It's too late to be angry!*~
I'm only telling you now because this is my last
chance.
You see.
I thought that it would be a sign.
A measure of what was meant to be.
I thought that if it was what we needed.
If a greater being had decided that it was what was
needed to be.
You know.
To make us be together.
Forever.

Then it would be.
I was putting it in the hands of a greater being.
It was out of my control.

[sound: distant rumbling of low flying aeroplane]

---

You see.
I love(*d*) you.
And I wasn't trying to trap you.
And I didn't want it to happen.
Want.
*Verb* + object.
Want a baby.

[silence]

Even if I had wanted.
I couldn't have planned.

[sound: a hoarse laugh]

---

*Verb:* To plan.
*Etymology:* French perhaps.
To map.
To scheme.
To arrange.
To plot.

---

I couldn't have planned for it to happen.

I've already said.

I can count the times on my right hand.

One.

Two.

Three.

I couldn't have planned it.

You had a problem with ejaculation.

*~Is that clear enough for you?~*

---

Ejaculation.

It's kind of a pretty sounding word.

*~Don't you think?~*

[sound: a guttural laugh]

[silence]

---

*Verb:* Ejaculate.

To eject words or sperm.

Not sperm.

Let me be proper.

Semen.

Spunk.

To release words.

To exclaim.

*Noun:* The thing that has been ejaculated.
The words or the spunky semen.
*Etymology:* of Latin origin.
Perhaps.
Ex/e being from or out.
And iaculari, to throw.
I think.
Perhaps.
Maybe.
It's a fine word.
It's a kind of pretty sounding word.
It's a letting it all come out kind of word.
   *~Am I making you uncomfortable?~*

[sound: creak of a wardrobe door]

---

But when it happened.
   *~When you ejaculated into me.~*
Well I had hope.
I had hope that we would begin a happily ever after.

[silence]

---

You won't know that I counted down the days till my period was due.
Of course you wouldn't know that.

33

You see.

I was existing in a haze.

In an exciting blur.

I was distracted.

I was often silent.

> *~I know that you didn't notice.~*

You never seemed to notice the signals that I sent to you.

Signals.

That implies a discreet code or gesture.

But even my boom boom booming signals weren't enough.

---

Boom.

Boom boom.

Boom.

Boom boom.

Boom boom boom.

[voiced: boom boom boom]

[volume: ↑ high ↓ low]

---

My period was due on 22nd March.

> *~How do I know?~*

I remember.

34

It was three days before my twenty-third birthday.

You were still twenty-two.

For another three months.

And you hated that I was older than you.

You said, **it isn't right**.

>       ~*Do you remember what you said?*~

You said, **the man should be older than the woman**.

You said, **my father was older than my mother**.

You said, **my grandfather was older than my grandmother**.

You said, **that's why I know that we aren't meant to be**.

And you said, **that's why we aren't quite right together**.

>       ~*Yes you did!*~

>       ~*I remember your words.*~

You told me that if God had intended for woman to be older than man.

Then he would have created Eve before Adam.

You liked that Eve was an appendage.

An afterthought.

It fitted.

It fitted with how you saw women.

An afterthought sent to lure and corrupt.

But I was older than you.

And that's why I didn't quite fit.

That's why you didn't quite slot into me.

>                            [sound: a guttural laugh]

---

Sue is younger than you.

*~Of course she is.~*

The tart is always younger.

Never older.

But she plays the role of the witch within this
twisted tale.

Let's call her Frau Gothel from now on.

*~I know that's not right.~*

I know that Frau Gothel should be older than me.

But this is my narrative.

And I get to cast the roles.

[sound: a guttural laugh]

Sue's six years younger than me.

*~I remember.~*

When she was eighteen she'd had a baby.

She'd had Lucy when she was eighteen years old.

*~I did the maths.~*

*~I used to be clever!~*

It was an easy sum.

It was an easy analysis.

You left me for a tart.

---

*~Don't you think that tart is a fine word?~*

It's light and sticky and sweet.

Not really an insult.

36

Now slag.

Slut.

Whore.

Witch.

Now if I called Sue any of those four words.

Then you could be insulted.

Then you'd have grounds to be insulted.

But I haven't.

>~Or have I?~

I can't remember.

[sound: water sloshing]

---

Tart.

Tartish.

>~Is that an adjective?~

Tartishly.

>~Is there such an adverb?~

A tart.

*Noun:* A pie.

A cake.

A topless sweet thing that you cover with your sweetness.

That you ejaculate onto.

*Noun:* A prostitute.

An immoral woman.

A wanton slag.
Sue.

[sound: a guttural laugh]

---

I didn't tell you about the countdown.
The countdown to the date that I expected to
be inserting tampons and cradling my cramping
stomach.
Expected.
That's a strange word.
It doesn't quite slot into the memory.
It jars.
It sticks out.
You see I didn't expect.
That's the whole point.
I didn't expect to see my period.
I knew.
I knew that I was pregnant.

> *~Or have I simply manipulated my memory
> into believing that I knew?~*

[voiced: blink blink]

[volume: low]

---

The countdown to my period lasted for twelve days.

My cycle was regular.

Twelve days from ejaculation to expected blood.

Like the twelve days of Christmas.

   *~That's a song isn't it?~*

You'd know the words.

I can't remember them all.

Just the five gold rings bit.

The words are slow and operatic.

[voiced: sings operatically five gold rings]

[volume: high]

---

Five golden rings.

Or five gold rings.

It makes a difference.

The gold or the golden.

*Adjective:* gold makes me assume that the rings are indeed made of gold.

*Adjective:* golden suggests a matter coloured gold, perhaps containing gold, but not necessarily being gold.

There's a difference.

A subtle yet noteworthy difference.

[sound: a loud sigh]

You should use five golden rings.

One for me.

One for Frau Gothel Sue.

And one for the next.

And one for the next after the next.

And one for the next after the next after the next.

They'd be flimsy and able to be snapped.

Nothing ever lasts.

Not for forever.

It just seems to go around and around and around
on the spot.

A ring.

A circle.

The ending and the beginning are one.

Moulded together.

---

I was due my period on a Friday.

*~Yes I remember everything.~*

You see I was in Newcastle that day.

I was buying my birthday present from you.

You'd given me twenty pounds to spend.

Twenty pound coins.

I was to buy something appropriate from you to me.

Because I was **difficult**.

Your word, not mine.

I think that you meant difficult to buy for.

And you said, **I am too busy**.

You were too busy with your PhD and your
university hours.
Too busy.
Busy.
Busy.
Busy.
I was **difficult**~...~
Elliptical construction noted.
Yet not fully understood.

[sound: a guttural laugh]

---

*Adjective:* Difficult.
Needing much planning.
Full of problems.
Trouble.
*Noun*: Ana.
Hard to tolerate.
Hard to comprehend.
Hard to unravel.
Hard to answer.
Hard to deal with.
Hard to fulfil.
Hard to cope with.
Hard to control.
Hard to please.

Hard to satisfy.

[sound: a guttural laugh]

Hard to convince.

Hard to persuade.

In considering what it is to be me.

I have become difficult.

Difficult has become Ana.

*~Highlight or tick the ones that apply!~*

*~Do I fulfil one?~*

*~Do I fulfil two three four?~*

*~Do I fulfil all of the above?~*

Perhaps now is the time to answer.

[sound: a guttural laugh]

---

The answer to my previous question should be
written on a postcard.

You'll need a stamp.

Remember to lick the stamp.

With your tongue.

Address it to ANA.

Not ALEX+ANA.

ANA in the black box.

Owner of the first golden ring.

The one that turned to dust.

The once keeper of a golden ring.

Until it crumbled with the pressure of her fingertips.
My fingers.

[sound: fingers clicking]

---

~*Am I being difficult?*~

I wouldn't say that I was.
I'd say that I was being pedantic.
Or even that I was being finicky.
Finicky is a nice word.
That can go onto my list of fine words.

[sound: scratching]

---

I remember that I was wandering around the city
centre.
Looking for something for me from you.
But I wasn't really focusing.
I wasn't really interested.
You see I was in a haze.
I was existing in that haze.
In an exciting blur.

~*I know that I've said that already!*~

I'm not brainless.

~*Or am I?*~

~*When did it happen?*~

*~Did I become brainless with motherhood?~*
*~Or did I become brainless when I*
*  abandoned my PhD?~*

---

Your twenty pound coins jingled in my jeans'
pocket.

[sound: rattle of coins within a china container]

I bought a round chocolate fudge cake from Marks
and Spencer.
And a bunch of yellow roses.
Yellow because you liked yellow.
Roses for love.
But not a single red rose of love.
A bunch of roses to show my love for you.
Not your love for me.
Because the thought that you'd ever love me was
funny.
That was a funny joke.

*~It still makes you laugh!~*

[sound: a snort]

---

[sound: a high-pitched scream]

Yellow.
The rose was once a symbol.

*~Once upon a time.~*

A rose was once a thing of love and devotion.

Lovers communicate(*d*) with flowers.

Those flowers carry their own language.

Colours and tone and words.

The language of flowers whispered words of
adoration to lovers across time.

[sound: a sigh]

The words that you whisper(*ed*) to me were in the
agglutinative language of Punjabi.

The adoration was stamped on by the subject.

Then the object.

Then the verb.

[sound: stamp stamp stamp foot to floor]

Our words were always yellow.

---

Shopping.

I was shopping.

My memory is sort of poor.

Backwards forwards, then round and round.

Shopping for me.

From you.

Because I was **difficult**.

*~Remember?~*

And everything that I bought for me from you was

from Marks and Spencer.

Because you liked fine things.

And they sold fine things.

And the twenty pound coins were almost gone.

The loose coins jingled in my jeans' pocket.

[sound: rattle of coins within a china container]

*~I'm setting the scene.~*

---

You were difficult to buy for.

*~Yes I know that I was buying for me!~*

But you were difficult to buy for, even when buying for me.

Your tastes were so precise.

So straight.

No creases.

No deviation.

Straight.

*~Why am I telling you all of this?~*

I'm setting the scene.

---

The scene: ANA shopping.

[sound: a guttural laugh]

---

Then I think that I wandered into a chemist.

> *~No I didn't wander.~*

I wouldn't have wandered.

I would have rushed.

I would have raced.

I would have been rapid.

I would not have wandered.

> [sound: stomping footsteps on carpeted floor]

And I bought a test.

The Test.

The holder of knowledge.

The answerer of questions.

It was in a blue box.

I remember being shocked by the price.

But I can't recall the price.

> *~I think that it was over five pounds.~*
>
> *~Maybe even six pounds!~*
>
> *~Or was it seven?~*

Funny how memory plays tricks.

> *~Not ha ha funny!~*
>
> *~Obviously.~*

Funny as in odd.

Strange.

Difficult.

It always comes back to **difficult**.

> *~Ok.~*

*~Ok!~*
*~I'll hurry the story along.~*

---

The Test was positive.
I was pregnant.

[silence]

---

Pregnant.
A momentous moment and/or being with child.
I have adapted the language to suit the context.
Context is everything.

---

*~Is my memory poor?~*
It works backwards.
The middle is the beginning is the end.

[sound: a sigh]

I had waited until I got home.
I did the Test in my flat.
I remember it being cold.
But it couldn't have been that cold.
It was nearly April.
I think that I was shaking.
I was shaking.

*~Yes I would have been shaking.~*

I would expect to be shaking.
In that scene.
In that moment.
I was shaking as I held the Test in my hands.
I was shaking as I fumbled with the plastic
packaging that wrapped around the Test.
I remember gripping the seal with my teeth and
tugging.
I remember being desperate to pee.
Desperate to know.

[five second silence]

That memory seems right.
That memory seems to fit.
~*Do you know that cold flurry of excitement
and nervousness?*~
Like on Christmas morning when you're a child.
You've hardly slept.
Your body is shaking.
Not cold shaking, just a nervous response.
A nervous energy that has combined with lack of
sleep.
The response is a shake.
A quiver.
A bottom lip tremble.
I remember the moment.
I had been waiting.

Counting down.

Eleven Ten Nine Eight Seven Six Five Four Three
Two One.

And then it was there.

The moment that seemed to take forever to arrive.

Well it arrived.

And I was almost too scared to know if he'd actually
been.

> *~Father Christmas of course!~*
> *~You don't believe in Father Christmas?~*
> *~You've never believed?~*
> *~Your mother didn't allow you to*
>   *fantasise?~*
> *~That explains a lot!~*

[sound: a guttural laugh]

---

You must have experienced that cold flurry of
excitement and nervousness.

> *~I know that you will have.~*

Fumbling in your wallet.

Checking in your wallet for a ripped out piece of
paper.

> *~You know what I'm talking about!~*

That moment just before you masturbated over her
image.

[sound: a guttural laugh]

---

I had read the instructions.

Then I had peed on the non-plastic end of the white
plastic stick.

Then I had perched on the edge of the bath.

> *~Do you remember my post-grad student*
> *bathroom?~*

It was exactly the width of the toilet and the small
white bath.

It was snug.

No shower.

Cream walls.

No window.

But it was always clean.

The toilet was never grubby.

But the ceiling was high.

I am remembering it being too high.

I couldn't even reach it when I balanced on the
bath.

I couldn't even reach it when I stretched out my
arm.

> *~No I'm not exaggerating!~*
> *~I remember!~*

You see.

The light bulb had blown and I couldn't reach to change it.

*~Or was it that I didn't have a spare?~*

I can't remember.

Anyway.

I remember that the bathroom door was open.

I remember looking through my legs and onto the Test.

I remember shuffling as my pee emerged to hit the Test.

Then I remember sitting on the edge of the bath.

My feet inside the bath.

No water in it.

And I remember clutching the pregnancy test and letting drips of my pee absorb into my fingers.

[sound: humming of same now vaguely recognisable tune]

---

I saw the strong blue line gush across the result's window.

There was no doubt.

A positive test.

I was pregnant.

And my response was to cry.

But the tears were warm.

They were happy tears.

I felt a surge of happiness.
I remember because the gush shocked me.
I smiled as the tears fell.
And then I wiped them away with my pee-steeped
fingers.

[sound: a muffled sob]

---

I phoned you.

    *~Do you remember the phone call?~*
    *~Do you remember how you reacted?~*
    *~Of course you don't.~*

You see it doesn't fit with the image of yourself that
you have perfected over the years.
The perfect father to Pip, Lucy, Davie and Kyle.
The perfect partner to Ana.
The perfect husband to Sue.
Flawless.
Straight.
Immaculate.
Sin-free and just.

[sound: a guttural laugh]

What you see is what you get.
A perfected image that doesn't quite fit.
I know that it doesn't quite fit, because I know the
real you.

I know that what you see is not what you get.

Not at all.

I know the twisted you.

I know the you that hides in the shadows and waits
for the dark of night to emerge.

[silence]

---

I know what you're capable of.

It still terrifies me.

But I have to be strong.

I haven't long.

This is what we both want.

[silence]

---

I remember the words that you spoke.

I remember what you did.

> ~*You can't forget!*~
> ~*Don't pretend that you can't hear me.*~
> ~*I won't let you forget!*~

[sound: banging of a wardrobe door]

> ~*Listen to me.*~
> ~*Please Alex.*~

I haven't long left.

[silence]

---

The telephone conversation.

It started with my usual, *hello*.

And my usual, *how are you?*

Then I cried.

*~I cried because I couldn't find the words.~*

Because I was frightened of the words.

You kept asking, **what's wrong?**

And I kept crying.

[sound: unrecognisable sound, perhaps a muffled sob]

And then you shouted into the receiver.

Demanding that I told you what was wrong.

Demanding.

The right verb is demanding.

[silence]

---

*Verb (used with object)*: Demand.

An urgent asking.

Demanding with authority.

Summoning.

Claiming a response.

*Etymology:* Old French.

I presume.

It may be derived from the Latin de, which in
this context could mean absolutely or totally and
mandare, meaning to order.

It was never a request.

I was never given a choice as to whether or not I replied.

It was required.

It was an obligation.

It was a requesting as a right.

A demand.

A demanding demand was demanded.

[sound: a guttural laugh]

---

~*Do you remember when I was clever?*~

I nearly had a PhD.

---

So.

You demanded.

And I had no choice but to say the words.

To speak the words into the telephone receiver.

I told you that I was pregnant.

[voiced: I'm pregnant]

[volume: low]

I just said the words.

~*I'm pregnant.*~

No other words.

And you said, **you must come around straight away.**

The must was a strong word.
It was one of your frequently used words.
A modal verb carrying obligation.
But that time it had a different edge to it.
Your voice had changed to being all sweet and soft.
It was a **you must** that spoke of my benefit from
doing so.
Rather than a **you must** that was a demand for your
own personal gain.
That's what it sounded like to me.
But my ears were full of water.

[sound: a guttural laugh]

---

I remember that I'd never heard that tone before
and I thought that you were happy.
That I had made you happy.
I hoped that your softness was warmth.
Mushiness.
I hoped that your green pea-sized heart had
mushed.
And I remember smiling to myself as I replaced the
telephone.
I remember thinking that everything was going to be
good.
To be fine.

To be happily ever after.

But happily ever after was never straightforward.

Happily ever after was never just around the corner.

---

*~Does happily ever after even exist?~*

*~Is it a state of mind?~*

It's not a physical condition.

It's not location specific.

It must be all in the mind.

It is all in the mind.

You see I live happily ever after.

*~I do!~*

When I look out from my black box.

And when I don't *blink*.

And when I don't scratch under my eyelids.

And when I live within the redness of my eyes.

Then I am within the happily ever after.

Within the happily ever after that was before the now and during the then.

I exist within the *blink* of a memory.

Within the *blink*.

Just after the first *blink*.

Of the *blink*.

*Blink blink.*

[voiced: blink blink]

58

[volume: low]

The memories are fading.

As the redness.

As the soreness envelops the memory.

I become trapped within the *blink*.

But I exist.

In the here.

In the now.

In the then.

In the when.

In between the end and the beginning.

I am trapped within this black box.

I live happily ever after.

> *~I do!~*

[silence]

---

So I walked to your flat.

In fact I practically flew.

The wings had sprouted from my back.

> *~Yes they had!~*

I remember the pain.

The scratching split as my skin opened for them to emerge.

I had white perfect feathers curving up to the sky.

> *~I did!~*

I managed a fifteen minute walk in eight minutes of flight.
My feet brushing the ground on every fifth leap.
And I brought the yellow roses and the round chocolate fudge cake with me.
Still within the Marks and Spencer carrier bag.
The handle was all wrinkled and crinkled.
My hands were sweaty from gripping it tightly through my journey.
And I hoped that you wouldn't mind that the bag that held your gift from you to me wasn't perfect.
My mind was a haze.
I had too much to think about.
I was on the brink of something.

[silence]

---

And you opened the door.
Before I pressed the bell.
You opened the door, just after I opened your wrought iron gate.

[silence]

---

The wrought iron gate.
It was twisted wrought iron.

Once red.

Twice black.

The thick paint broadened the bars.

I love(*d*) that gate.

It hung with a lopsided tilt.

The bottom of the gate trailed along the ground,

leaving a faint black mark along your cracked

pathway.

The rusted hinges creaked.

The scraping noise warned you.

Prepared you for visitors.

> *~Why did you like to be prepared?~*
> *~Why did you need to be warned?~*

One day it would fall to the ground.

I knew that each time that I pushed the gate.

That one time it would be the last.

That one day the hinges would separate.

They would crumble.

They would dissolve to dust.

And the twisted wrought iron, with the thick paint

broadening the bars would fall to the ground.

[sound: foot banging on the ground]

But I never saw that happen.

You had moved on.

*~And do you remember what you did?~*

I don't understand why I remember and you don't.

I often wonder if you have altered the events within your memory.

Or if the memory even exists.

Record.

Retain.

Recall.

It should be straightforward.

No twists, no kinks.

*~Does the memory exist?~*

My memories go backwards forwards.

You see.

The words are crisp and fresh.

My memory is precise.

But.

I don't know if it is accurate.

I don't know if my memory is working.

*~How can I test to see if my memory is working?~*

[silence]

_____

When you opened the door you hugged me.

I can see a me and a you.

In between the twisted wrought iron gate, with the

thick paint broadening the bars and your front door.

*~What colour was your front door?~*

I can't remember.

My memory plays trickery.

Its illusions confuse me.

I remember the hug.

I can see the hug.

I can recall the tightness.

My body was stiff in reaction.

And your arms gripped around me.

All the way around.

Tightly.

Forcing down the arms of a me.

A me holding a Marks and Spencer carrier bag.

And I remember crying into you.

The memory carries a sensation.

A dampness.

Coldness on my cheeks.

I can still feel it.

The smell of sandalwood and drugs.

I can still smell you.

And then you said, **everything is going to be ok**.

And you said it in those ailing soft and sugary tones.

And the tone had warmth.

A mushiness that I didn't recognise, at that time.

I have since learned to consider it with revulsion.

[sound: a guttural laugh]

But your front door.

That front door.

> *~Was there glass?~*

I must keep this image simple.

No glass.

No glass.

> *~Was the door an inky blue?~*

I don't think so.

I can't remember.

I can't recall.

The colour has been *blink*ed away.

Let's say that it was red.

Let me fill in the colour.

[five second silence]

The memory needs to be perfect.

> *~What good is a memory if it is not perfect?~*

Perfection.

I must not *blink* again.

---

You use those ailing soft and sugary tones with me now.

Every now and then.

When we speak on the telephone.

> *~When we have to speak on the telephone.~*

You stopped coming to see me.

I caused one fuss too many.

I embarrass(*ed*) you.

One time too many.

I disgust(*ed*) you.

My body.

My smell.

My look.

They all cause **repulsion**.

Your word not mine.

[sound: sobbing]

If you sniff into my armpit.

If you nuzzle your nose into my soft hairs.

You will smell you.

The water within my body is full of you.

The secretions are as you try to escape.

*~Go on sniff yourself back.~*

I still have you within me.

[sound: sniff sniff sniff]

_____

You stopped coming in to my flat.

You arranged to pick the children up from downstairs.

From outside.

From out of my view.

I can't see you from here.
I don't like to leave my black box.
I have no reason to leave it.
But.
Sometimes you telephone and you must speak to
me.
And you use those ailing soft and sugary tones.
Your tone is soft and warm.
You pretend to care.
        *~You were always good at pretending.~*
Because there is always a reason for your telephone
call.
There is always a need within your telephone
contact with me.
Gain.
You seek to gain.
The gain is never mine.
I have nothing to gain.
I have nothing outside of this black box.
My children exist within my memories.
They are no longer real.
They died.
        *~I know that they still breathe.~*
They died within my life.
They exist within memories that I prefer not to visit.
You left.

You left us all.
I cannot recall memories after you left.
I choose not to force them.
I cannot open the door.
I cannot communicate outside of my box.
This box.
My black box.

> *~Can you hear my words?~*

[silence]

---

> *~Am I trapped?~*
> *~Do I have an alternative?~*
> *~Is there a resolution to be found?~*

The door is closed.
But it will open.
I could open it.
The window has locks.
They are not fastened.
I could open them.

[sound: a yawn]

But I am trapped.
Trapped within the visuals.
Performing within memories.
Experiencing the rawness of emotions from events
that should be buried.

That will soon be buried.

In a grave.

With me.

~*With us.*~

[sound: sobbing]

But you did come back.

You came back tonight.

You came back to kill me.

_____ _____

I need to sleep.

[fifteen second silence]

_____

The memory.

This lack of structure is worrying.

I have altered my way of being.

End.

Middle.

Beginning.

Beginning.

End.

Middle.

The working backwards endwards, forwards,
middlewards.

It is somewhat distressing.

The memory was paused within the visual of a me
and a you.

In between the twisted wrought iron gate, with the
thick paint broadening the bars and your red front
door.

*~Was your front door red?~*

[silence]

We are motionless.

A single breath will gust us over.

Us.

[sound: a loud sigh]

But.

I can't recall the weather.

I can't recall the sky.

[voiced: my memory is falling]

[volume: low]

Let's say that it was red.

That the clouds were red in the pale blue sky.

Details are often insignificant in the backward
workings from here to somewhere before there.

And.

Let's say that your arms wrapped around me.

That's a true fact.

I can feel the sensation.

My stiff body and rigidly straight arms by my side.

And that was when you told me, **everything is going**

**to be ok**.

[voiced: everything is going to be ok]

[volume: low]

In warm tones.

In what I believed to be warm tones.

I believed it then.

I don't now.

~*Or do I?*~

Perhaps I do.

I still think of those ailing soft and sugary tones.

I sometimes enjoy them within the memory.

But.

And there is always at least one but with you.

Then you said that, **everything will be fine**.

And then you said, **abortions are practically routine these days**.

[voiced: abortion]

[volume: high]

And that was when I pulled out of the tight tight hug.

~*Do you remember those words?*~
~*Any of those words?*~

[voiced: abortion abortion abortion]

[volume: high]

An abortion.

Abortion is a red word.

It brings red.

Red seeps out from each letter and it drip drops to the floor.

It makes the view from here red.

---

*Noun:* Abortion.

*Etymology:* I can't remember.

>                    *~Why can't I remember?~*

The termination of a pregnancy through the removal of a foetus or embryo.

The noun drips red before my eyes.

Abortion or abortive.

Perhaps I can't recall the etymology because the adjective came first.

I am focusing on the noun.

I know the word abortus.

It is the past participle of aborire.

I believe that it means to disappear.

But then I recall aborire meaning to miscarry.

Past participle.

>                    *~Am I making up words now?~*

Words sound familiar.

They roll from my tongue.

Meaning seems to be lost.
I am not what I once was.

[silence]

---

You knew everything about me.
> ~*You used to know everything about me.*~

About the me before I was the +ANA in ALEX+ANA.
It was a consequence of being friends first.
So you knew.
You knew that I had had an abortion.
After man number seven.
Three days before man number eight.
I didn't wait.
The intercourse with man number eight, ended with
his cock dripping my terminated foetus' blood.
Onto my stomach.
I had wanted to be back to normal.
I had wanted to be normal, to pretend that the
abortion had never happened.
That was when I knew normal.
When I could recognise my normal self.
I sometimes wonder if I love that dead foetus more
than I do my own breathing children.

[six second silence]

You knew that I had been pregnant before.

And that I'd decided not to have that baby.

That foetus.

That foetus was sucked out of me.

[sound: a sucking noise]

And you knew that I'd just gotten on with the whole thing.

On my own.

Without making a fuss or protest.

I never liked commotion.

And you probably saw my actions as calculated and cold.

I didn't think.

I didn't consider before the event.

And then afterwards there was nothing that I could do.

[sound: sobbing]

[volume: high]

---

I'd had an abortion.

Just like I'd had a packet of crisps.

And I'd had a cold.

And I'd had my purse stolen when I was sightseeing in Trafalgar Square.

*~Have I ever been to London?~*

[sound: a guttural laugh]

---

Context.

It is always about context.

A single form, a lexical item can function differently depending on the context and often the co-text.

Traditional word class categories are often too rigid when analysing in relation to context.

The key is to provide as much contextual information as possible.

And I am giving you the context.

The pragmatics are there to be considered.

~*A hide and seek of meaning?*~

The words and sounds and the silence combine.

The picture is created.

You see.

Abortion is a red raw word.

It scrapes and then it scabs.

And red oozes from it.

Even when it appears to heal.

It never heals.

[sound: scratching]

*Noun:* Abortion.

*Etymology:* I need to remember.

*Etymology:* I can't recall.

I really am confused.

Abortion or abortive.

Perhaps I can't recall because the adjective came first.

I am focusing on the noun.

A noun.

That noun.

> *~Is it important?~*
>
> *~Does it alter the meaning?~*

The termination: the termination of a pregnancy
through the removal of a foetus or embryo.

> *~Do I need the etymology to continue with
> the narrative?~*

You see.

I see the word abortion.

If I don't *blink*.

If I stare out from my black box.

I see the word.

ABORTION.

Curved lines next to straight lines.

Written in the sand.

---

> *~Do you remember that I stayed the night?~*

After you told me to have an abortion.

I stayed the night.

I smoked your joints.

And I drank your wine.

And we ate my round chocolate fudge cake.

Even though it was not my birthday.

You had the munchies.
You were eating for two.

[sound: a guttural laugh]

The chocolate layered the top of my mouth.
My dry dry mouth.
And then you picked the petals from my ten long-
stemmed yellow roses.
You scattered and spread my yellow curled petals
across your grubby floor.

---

He loves me.
    ~*He loves me not.*~
He loves me.
    ~*He loves me not.*~
He loves me.
    ~*He loves me not.*~
He loves me.
    ~*He loves me not.*~
He loves me.
    ~*He loves me not.*~
He loves me.
    ~*He loves me not.*~
He loves me.
    ~*He loves me not.*~
He loves me.

    *~He loves me not.~*

He loves me.

    *~He loves me not.~*

He loves me.

    *~He loves me not.~*

[sound: sobbing]

---

    *~Do you remember our spending the night*
      *together?~*

    *~Or that you entered me?~*

That you tried to thrust the baby away.

You were hard.

You were too hard.

Your actions were vigorous.

Sharp.

Painful.

We did not talk about my being pregnant.

    *~Do you remember that we did not talk*
      *about my being pregnant?~*

    *~How can you remember something that*
      *didn't exist?~*

Your memory now exists without me in there.

I am a smear.

Wiped.

Not quite clean.

Caroline Smailes

[sound: a guttural laugh]

You slept.

I didn't.

I couldn't.

---

*~Do you remember waking in the morning?~*

You looked at me.

And with your morning breath.

You told me, **fuck off**.

Your words, not mine.

You told me, **don't contact me again until you've got rid of the baby.**

You used the word **rid**.

It's a sharp word.

I dressed.

With tears and snot streaming down my face.

*~Do you remember?~*

I can see myself.

I can see a hunched me.

Sobbing.

Breathing sharp.

Not speaking.

Fumbling for my clothes within the darkness of your bedroom.

[sound: sobbing]

You were still in bed.
The sheets wrapped around your smooth nakedness.
Your back was to me.
And I left your flat.
I left you within the crumpled sheets.

[sound: distant rumbling of low flying aeroplane]

---

You see I had had an abortion before.
You knew that.
But you didn't know that the baby that I had killed
haunted my dreams.
Arms missing.
An eye missing.
I heard his crying before I saw his twisted being.

[sound: sobbing]

And I knew.
I knew from the moment that the positive blue line
appeared on the test.
I could not abort another child.
I had no right to abort another child.
Consequences for actions.
I was determined to accept my fate.
My baby.

[voiced: my pip]

[volume: low]

And there was nothing that you could say or do that would alter this.

Another abortion was not an option.

> *~You didn't know that did you?~*

But you never asked.

You never asked the questions.

You didn't care to ask.

Words were not significant.

So instead of contacting the campus doctor.

I telephoned a Pro Life organisation.

And I cried down the telephone.

[sound: sobbing]

And they said that they would help me.

That they would help me to say no to you.

And that they would speak to me.

That they would be there for me.

> *~Yes I told them about you and about what you wanted me to do!~*
>
> *~Yes I even told them your name!~*

I remember being sure that I could hear the lady taking notes.

That I could hear her pencil jotting onto a pad.

I called her from a payphone.

My back sliding down the glass.

As I spoke to her into the phone.

I could hear her scribbling down my words.

[sound: scribbling on paper]

Your name.

It is within a file.

Within my file.

You see I had to tell someone.

I needed to talk to someone.

They could only be contacted between the hours of 11am and 1pm.

And I contacted them during those hours.

---

I fought with myself.

I forced myself to stay away from you.

I stopped myself from phoning you.

Well that's not exactly true.

*~But you know that don't you?~*

I couldn't stop myself from pressing the buttons and phoning you.

You were my obsession.

My habit.

And the panic grew and grew inside me.

I'd sit next to the telephone willing it to ring.

But it didn't.

You had no intention of telephoning me.

You didn't need to hear my voice.

I needed to hear yours.

I needed to know what you were doing.

I needed you to be thinking about me.

I was filled with panic.

[sound: a sharp intake of air]

And the panic grew and grew.

And somehow in amongst the panic, I justified my need to telephone you.

I allowed myself to press your numbers.

The pads of my fingers functioned automatically.

And I would call just to hear your voice.

Just for the, **hello**.

For your, **hello**.

[voiced: hello]

[volume: low]

And then I would hang up.

My fingertip poised.

Quivering over the button.

[sound: humming of same now vaguely recognisable tune]

You changed your number after three weeks.

[sound: a throaty laugh]

*~Well you didn't did you?~*

Your mother did it for you.

Your mother did everything for you.

Let me remind you of the story.

### ~*Are you sitting comfortably?*~

It was the you and me story at that time.

The ALEX+ANA story.

Then your mother stepped in.

Penny Edwards-Knight.

[silence]

---

Your mother.

I can't find a definition that fits.

I have no idea what a mother is supposed to be.

I have no mother.

[sound: distant rumbling of low flying aeroplane]

---

I have read somewhere.

I have heard somewhere.

It is blurred.

My memory is blurred.

But the relationship that a man has with his mother
is an indicator.

A flashing red light.

A signal.

For something.

But I don't know what that something is.

I can't remember.

*~Help me to remember.~*
*~Please.~*

[silence]

---

Your mother.
We had been together for three years and I had not met her.
I asked about her.
I heard you speak to her on the phone.
And I'd ask questions.
About you and her.
But you didn't want to tell me.

*~Am I making you feel uncomfortable?~*

You'd tell me the curriculum vitae stuff.
But if I questioned the relationship that you shared.
You'd tell me, **my mother is nothing to do with you**.
You'd tell me, **my mother is my ideal woman**.

[voiced: ideal woman]

[volume: low]

Those words have stuck.
You'd tell me, **my mother is everything that I could hope for within a woman.**

*~That's a bit odd really.~*
*~Don't you think?~*
*~Of course I am not making this up!~*

84

I should have delved into that a bit more.
But I didn't.
I can't believe that I was that stupid.
So for three years I didn't meet her.
I feared her instead.

-----

*~Did you have sex with your mother?~*
*~Did she make you thrust into her until she*
*came all over your cock?~*
I often wonder(*ed*).
I have my suspicions.

[voiced: unrecognisable words]

[volume: low]

-----

Your mother had divorced your father when you
were three years old and your sister five.
She still kept the Edwards, but added a Knight to
form a double barrel.
*~Yes I know that you know these details!~*
Your mother had divorced your father because she
preferred being single.
She wanted to do as she pleased.
She didn't want to answer to anyone else.
It wasn't about sex.

It wasn't about the double barrel.
Or so you told me.
And from the day of her divorce.
From the stories and details that I have grabbed.
Well your mother planned out every aspect of both
yours and your sister's lives.
Your life was to be straight.
A straight line from here to there.
I was a pot hole.
A black tumbling hole.
And when she said jump.
You did.
Right over me.

[voiced: unrecognisable word]

[volume: low]

---

Your mother was an academic.
Penny Edwards-Knight, the academic.
She travelled the country with a pharmaceutical
company.
And was paid a yearly fee by them.
A fee.
I love(*d*) that you called it a fee.
It made it sound so insignificant.

*~It wasn't though was it?~*

86

She was a consultant.

A researcher.

An academic who was easily bought.

Her opinions altered to suit the drug that she was being paid to promote.

And as you'd boast details about your high-flying goddess.

I'd think of her as a chameleon.

A scaly, hard-skinned reptile who changed to fit with her environment.

A crusty reptile slinking around dragging a huge sack of gold behind her.

I hated your mother before I even met her.

---

I hated your mother when I met her.

The feeling was mutual.

I could see it in her eyes.

I could hear it twist from her tongue

> *~Did she ever wrap you up with her tongue?~*

---

Your mother.

Ms Penny Edwards-Knight.

She demanded attention.

She demanded.

And for hours before she telephoned, you would practise your backwards language.

You spoke every word to her backwards.

Not forwards.

The language that she demanded you communicate in.

> *~Do you still use it?~*

For the hours leading up to the designated phone call time, you'd refuse to speak to me.

The hours were for you to rehearse, to perfect your backward mother tongue.

And every first Sunday of the month.

Between the hours of one and three.

Your mother expected a long and thorough telephone conversation highlighting the key points of the previous month.

In backward tongue.

You made notes.

Of course you made notes.

> *~Didn't you realise that I knew about your scribbled points to include in a conversation?~*

Theme.

Rheme.

Theme.

Rheme.

You made meticulous notes in the black notebook.

Your little black book.

She bought you a new one each Christmas.

[sound: a throaty laugh]

[silence]

---

And each Christmas you wrapped the filled
notebook of notes.

For her.

Tied it with a red shiny bow.

For her.

[silence]

---

ruoy rehtom.

ehS dednamed noitnetta.

ehS dednamed.

dnA rof sruoh erofeb ehs denohpelet uoy dluow
esitcarp ruoy sdrawkcab egaugnal.

ehT egaugnal taht ehs dednamed uoy etacinummoc
ni.

*~Do you still use it?~*

roF eht sruoh gnidael pu ot eht detangised enohp
llac emit, d'uoy esufer ot kaeps ot em.

ehT sruoh erew rof uoy ot esraeher, ot tcefrep ruoy
drawkcab rehtom eugnot.

dnA yreve tsrif yadnuS fo eht htnom.

neewteB eht sruoh fo eno dna eerht.

ruoY rehtom detcepxe a gnol dna hguoroht
enohpelet noitasrevnoc gnithgilhgih eht yek stniop
fo eht suoiverp htnom.

nI drawkcab eugnot.

uoY edam seton.

fO esruoc uoy edam seton.

> ~Didn't you realise that I knew about
> your scribbled points to include in a
> conversation?~

uoY edam suolucitem seton ni eht kcalb koobeton.

ruoY elttil kcalb koob.

ehS thguob uoy a wen eno hcae samtsirhC.

dnA hcae samtsirhC uoy depparw eht dellif
koobeton fo seton.

roF reh.

---

> ~So where does she step in?~

Step in.

> ~Is that dramatic enough?~

It was more like a leap with both feet flying into my
stomach.

[sound: distant rumbling of low flying aeroplane]

[sound: banging]

---

It was almost four weeks after you told me to have an abortion.

[voiced: abortion]

[volume: low]

The story goes that your mother was visiting Newcastle.
Because you weren't from Newcastle.
You were born in a house in a village.
In a village called Mortney.
A village lost in between Liverpool and Chester.
A village where people spoke in money.

[voiced: sings money money money]

[volume: high]

And your community clung to a village hall that was thatched in gold.
And a church, where the preacher was at least one hundred and seven.
Your neighbours fasted for twenty-four hours before communion.
And the preacher spoke in repeated riddles.
Chastising those who orgasm outside of marriage.
I know because he baptised Pip.

*~Do you remember?~*
He talked of whores and entrapment whilst
splashing water on Pip's head.
I still quiver.

[sound: splashing water]

---

Backwards forwards sideways memory.
*~Where are my tablets?~*
*~Where are my tablets?~*

[sound: high-pitched scream]

[silence]

---

The story goes that your mother was in Newcastle.
Your mother had been giving one of her seminars
and she had expected you to meet her for dinner.
It had been a definite date that had been made on
the first Sunday of that month.
Of April.
After the pregnancy test.
And you had stood her up.
And that was so very out of character.
Away from your assumed role in her performance.

[sound: a guttural laugh]

You did not jilt your mother.

No one did that.

Your mother did not **abide** such behaviour.

**Abide**.

One of your words.

Not mine.

---

The story continues.

She had driven to your flat.

I don't know how long she had waited for you.

I don't know where you were supposed to meet her.

> *~Isn't it odd how some details never lock*
> *into a memory?~*

I wouldn't have overheard the conversation.

And even if I had overheard the backward tongue.

I did not speak your language.

You knew that.

That's why you **permitted** my being in the same
room.

**Permitted**.

One of your words.

Not mine.

And when your mother telephoned, I would sit in
silence.

If you could have stopped me breathing every first

Sunday of the month.

Between the hours of one and three.

Then you would have.

[sound: unrecognisable, perhaps muffled sob]

I was always silent when your mother called.

She was never to know that I was there.

[silence]

---

I am aware that soon you will have stopped me breathing.

*~Is it the first Sunday of the month?~*

[silence]

---

Your mother had arrived at your flat and she had found that your curtains were closed.

And that you were not answering your telephone.

And so.

I returned from university and your mother telephoned me.

*~How did she get my telephone number?~*

I've never asked that before.

I don't think that I have.

*~Have I asked that before?~*

[voiced: my memory is falling]

94

[volume: low]

---

I remember hearing her voice for the first time.

It was gravelly.

A smoker's voice.

> *~Did she smoke then?~*

In my memory, I picture her with a long thin
cigarette holder.

Elegant and white.

With her hands always gloved.

My memory is not as it once was.

[voiced: my memory is falling]

[volume: low]

I fill in the holes.

> *~Does that lessen the value of the memory?~*

The lines have blurred.

Your mother told me that you hadn't met her.

She shouted at me that you hadn't met her.

Your mother told me that she was sitting outside my
flat in her car.

She told me that she was desperate to use the little
girl's room.

I call it a toilet.

She must have been outside my flat when I came in.

She must have watched me come in.

*~Had you described me to her?~*
*~What words had you used?~*
*~Were they backwards mother tongue*
*words?~*
She asked if she could come into my flat.
And use my little girl's room.
I had never met her before.
You had never wanted me to meet her.
She had never wanted to meet me.
*~What could I say?~*
I couldn't let your mother pee in her pants.
And I guess that I was curious.
That I was hopeful.
I hoped that she might fall in love with me.
And that you would then have to fall in love with
me too.
Because your mother told you to.
*~But how did she know where I lived?~*
I've never asked you that before.
I don't think I have.
I have so many unanswered questions.

[voiced: my memory is falling]

[volume: low]

---

So I buzzed your mother into my flat.

She didn't ask which number.

> *~How did she know which number and*
> *which floor?~*

I don't know the answers.

They weren't significant then.

But with this recall there are too many holes.

Memory alters the focus.

As your mother climbed the two floors to reach my flat.

I just had time to put bleach into the toilet.

And to put some cheap gel into my too short hair.

And then she was there.

Banging on my door.

It was a clenched fist on my door kind of bang.

[sound: fist bang bang banging on wood]

[volume: high]

> *~Do you know all of this?~*
> *~Stop me if I am boring you!~*

[sound: exaggerated yawn]

[volume: high]

---

I opened the door.

I feared that she would bang it down with her fist.

[sound: stomping footsteps on carpeted floor]

Your mother came in.

The toilet was directly in front of her.
She looked past me and to the toilet.
She walked past me and to the toilet.
> *~Did she shove me out of the way with her*
> *padded shoulder?~*
> *~I don't think that she spoke a hello.~*
In my memory she didn't speak.
In my memory she shoved past me and I staggered
backwards.

[voiced: my memory is falling]

[volume: low]

But I remember the feeling of dread.
It was a sweeping wave that left a clammy tack, as
I remembered that the light wasn't working in my
toilet.
I still hadn't changed the bulb.
I hadn't bought another bulb.
Or perhaps it was that I still couldn't reach the light
socket.
I can't remember.
> *~Do I need to remember?~*

[silence]

Your mother fumbled for the switch.
And the light didn't flick.
And she turned to speak to me.
She asked if I had not paid my electricity bill.

Her red eyes burned into me.

> *~They were red weren't they?~*
> *~I remember her having red eyes that burned*
> *through my flesh.~*

I remember telling her that I couldn't reach the light socket.

I remember thinking that I would light the candle in the toilet.

I walked past her, brushing the backs of my knees against the bath so as not to touch her.

I used a lighter that was running low on fuel.

The wheel was stiff and wouldn't ignite.

I was fumbling.

Your mother watched.

I can still feel her glare and stare.

I could sense that she wasn't impressed.

[sound: lighter being ignited six times]

And as I lit the candle on top of the cistern, I knew that she was watching me.

I could feel her red eyes burning into my flesh.

> *~Yes she did!~*

I remember turning.

I remember not catching her eye.

I walked by.

She gave a sigh and a tut.

[sound: a tut]

[sound: a sigh]

[volume: high]

And I am sure that her tail swished under her long flowing skirt as she closed the bathroom door.

---

Your mother peed in my toilet.

I could hear her through the paper thin walls.

A continuous stream of pee.

Then the noise of the toilet roll spinning within the holder.

And she came out.

She did not wash her hands.

[silence]

I did not offer her a drink.

*~Why should I have offered her a drink?~*

I didn't want her to stay.

I wanted her to go.

She filled my flat.

She made my flat seem small.

I was suffocating.

Her silence was choking me.

Her silence was tightening around my throat.

She watched.

She absorbed.

She stole.

*~I am not exaggerating!~*
*~Don't look at me like that!~*

In my memory I am a fading me, as she sucked the essence of me from my body.

But then she asked me where you were.

And I said that I didn't know.

And she said that she didn't understand.

And I said that I hadn't spoken to you for almost four weeks.

I didn't say that I hadn't heard your voice.

Because I had.

I just told her that I hadn't spoken to you and I kind of stressed the spoken a little too much.

And she didn't ask why.

*~Did she know why?~*
*~Had you told her why?~*

And then she told me that she was really worried about you.

And the way that she spoke the word really, gave it an emphasis that caused alarm bells to ding dong ding inside my head.

With that single adverb she was telling me that she thought that you might have harmed yourself.

But she didn't use the words.

I could never say that she used the words self-harm or even suicide.

The words were within the stressed adverb.
The implication carried such intensity.
Such heaviness.

[sound: sigh]

[volume: high]

---

So I panicked.
Your mother made me panic.
I felt sick.
And in my memory the colour faded from my
cheeks and my knees buckled.
The words came blurting out.
I told her.
I told her, *I'm pregnant*.

[voiced: I'm pregnant]

[volume: low]

---

~*Did your mother really pee into my toilet?*~
I don't know.
I thought that I heard your mother peeing in my
toilet.
I thought that I could hear her through the paper
thin walls.
I thought that I heard a continuous stream of pee.

I thought that I heard the noise of the toilet roll
spinning within the holder.
I don't know.

[voiced: my memory is falling]

[volume: low]

But I do remember that your mother didn't wash her
hands.
I think I remember.

[sound: sigh]

[volume: high]

Perhaps she didn't pee.
Perhaps she was masturbating instead.

[sound: a guttural laugh]

Perhaps she was flicking two fingers over her
clitoris.

[sound: sniffing]

---

Your mother smiled at me.

[silence]

I'll never forget that smile.
She said that she wasn't surprised.
And then she asked if she could use my telephone.
She called your sister.
I only know because it wasn't your sister who
answered the telephone.

She had to ask for your sister.
And then she began to talk in her backwards
language.
And I could only catch one or two words.
I stopped listening.
I stopped trying to decode.
I walked into the kitchen.
And I stood not making your mother a cup of
coffee.

[voiced: blink blink]

[volume: low]

---

Your mother ended her telephone conversation.
I remember re-entering the room.
And I remember her turning to me.
I remember her staring with her red red eyes.
And she told me that she thought it best if I drove
with her.
If we tried to find you.
And I agreed.
Because I didn't know what else to say.
Because I wanted to see you.
Because I needed to know that I hadn't made you
kill yourself.
I remember the panic.

A panic that made me forget to breathe.
A panic that made me want to walk around and
around in a circle.
Your mother was calm.
We got into her car.
In my memory it is silver.

> *~Was it silver?~*
> *~Does it matter if it wasn't?~*

I don't know.
I keep *blink*ing.

[voiced: blink blink]

[volume: low]

---

> *~And do you know where she drove me to?~*
> *~You do.~*
> *~Of course you do!~*

She couldn't have planned it all so quickly.
That bit of the memory doesn't fit.
I used to think that your mother had returned the
next day.
But she hadn't.
Within my memory we are wearing the same
clothes.
And I have thought about this.
From within this black box.

And there is only one possible answer.

You must have given her help.

You must have told her.

You must have told her that I was pregnant.

You must have told her your problem.

> *~I am right aren't I?~*

I am trying to fill in the holes.

I am filling in the bits that are grey.

I am adding the colours.

---

> *~What language did you use when you spoke*
> *to your mother?~*

I need to know.

When you told her that I was pregnant.

When you pushed the blame onto me.

> *~Which language did you use?~*

I know that you told her.

You must have told her.

Nothing else makes sense.

> *~Admit it!~*

> *~Go on admit it!~*

> *~Please.~*

> *~Please tell me.~*

You see that memory doesn't fit.

I can't fill the holes.
Something isn't right.
>*~Tell me.~*
>*~I need to know.~*
I need to know before it is too late.
>*~Did you wait until the first Sunday of the*
>    *month?~*
>*~Was it between the hours of one and*
>    *three?~*
Your mother would have expected a long and
thorough telephone conversation highlighting the
key points of the previous month.
In backward tongue.
I must be in one of your notebooks.
I must have been part of a Christmas gift to her that
very year.
>*~Am I lost within your backward tongue*
>    *notes?*
>*~Am I there?~*
I must be there.
anA si tnangerp.
There must be details of Ana being with child.
Ana gnieb htiw dlihc.

>                                   [voiced: I'm pregnant]
>                                   [volume: low]

>*~Tell me.~*

*~Give me the words.~*
This is my final chance to fill in the holes.
I don't have long.

*~But you know that don't you?~*

---

I remember climbing into the passenger seat of your
mother's silver car.

*~Let's keep the car as silver.~*
I remember the lack of words.
She drove without words.
Silence.

[five second silence]

I remember that your mother did not drive to your
flat.
And I remember wondering if she was lost.
Instead.
Your mother drove me to a mansion.
A mansion with huge wrought iron gates.
And with huge green bushes and trees that bordered
a long curved driveway.

[voiced: I'm pregnant]

[volume: low]

Your mother drove me up the driveway that was
lined with green.
And before I realised where we were and why we

were there and what was there, I was in a perfectly
square room with a high ceiling.
There are holes in this memory.

[silence]

I remember film set furnishings and fabrics from
costume dramas surrounded me.
They made me smile.
I remember a polished grand piano in the right
corner and bookcases of perfectly bound unread
books lined the left wall.
I remember your mother perched on the edge
of a walnut spoon-backed nursing chair, sipping
cappuccino from a white cup.
I remember thinking that she was rude for not
having offered me a drink.
And then my name was called.

---

I remember that my full name was called.
*Anabel Lewis.*
I remember because it shocked me.
It was loud and echoed around the spacious room.

[voiced: anabel lewis]

[volume: high]

I was seeing a private doctor.
In a private clinic.

In a mansion with huge wrought iron gates to keep
people in and out.
The doctor was being paid with private money.
Your mother's money.
And that doctor with his sack full of your mother's
money, was ready and keen to suck your baby out
of me.
To suck your Pip out of me.

[voiced: my pip]

[volume: low]

> *~Do you know all of this?~*
> *~Did she report it back to you?~*

You never mentioned it.
We never discussed it.

---

I remember that I stood to follow the nurse into an
examining parlour.
I remember that your mother didn't stand.
Your mother didn't come in with me.
She had her cappuccino in a white cup and a copy
of *Tatler* to read.

> *~Ok so perhaps I am being creative with the*
> *magazine title, but it fits.~*

Your mother didn't need to be a part of the actual
abortion.

110

*~Yes abortion!~*

The nurse was smiley.

Too smiley.

I remember that I didn't sit on the Victorian nursing chair.

I stood.

> *~I can't remember what colour the chair*
> *was.~*
> *~Do I need to remember what colour the*
> *chair was?~*

I know that I told the doctor that I didn't want an abortion.

I told the doctor that I was 23 years old and ready to have a child.

It wasn't dramatic.

It wasn't a climax-building scene.

I didn't have to find my voice a split second before the drugs were being administered.

The doctor's first question asked if I consented to the termination.

And I said, *no*.

And then I outlined my reasons why.

[voiced: abortion abortion abortion]

[volume: high]

*One abortion is too many in a woman's life.*

I was articulate.

I still had a mind.

Then.

I was clear.

Then.

I knew that I wanted the baby.

Then.

And no doctor and no sack of money were going to suck my baby from me.

[sound: humming of same now vaguely recognisable tune]

So I told the doctor that I had had an abortion before.

After man number seven.

Three days before man number eight.

I told the doctor that in my mind that dead foetus breathed as a child.

I told the doctor that I longed for that child.

The aborted foetus.

[six second silence]

That foetus.

That foetus that was sucked out of me.

[sound: a sucking noise]

I think I told him all of this.

I am getting confused.

~*Did I tell you this or the doctor?*~

~*I know that you're a doctor too.*~

~*You're not a medical doctor though.*~

112

*~Please stop confusing me!~*

I think that maybe I told the doctor that the regret
and guilt and longing cover me.

*~I don't care if I've said that before.~*

It needs saying.

It needs voicing again.

[sound: sobbing]

This is my chance to repent.

---

*~Have you heard this before?~*

I must have finished my articulation.

And I think that the doctor nodded.

I think that I needed to sit.

I remember a wave of nausea.

In my memory I feel nauseous.

*~Was that when my morning sickness
began?~*

The doctor spoke to the nurse quickly and in
slightly hushed tones.

I didn't catch the words.

I don't think that I tried to listen.

Then the nurse showed me out of the clinic by a
different door.

A backdoor.

And I left your mother sitting in the private waiting

area with her cappuccino in a white cup.

I wonder how long she waited.

> *~Did she ever tell you?~*
> *~Can you fill in the holes for me now?~*
> *~Please tell me all that you know.~*

[sound: a guttural laugh]

---

I was eleven weeks pregnant when you contacted
me again.

> *~Was everything planned in advance?~*
> *~Did you count the weeks and the days and
> the hours before contacting me again?~*

I did.

[silence]

I need to sleep.

I need to sleep now.

I fear that this may be it.

I may not wake again.

[sound: sobbing]

[silence]

---

# BLACK
# BOX #02

> > > > >

**[55°02'24.58" N 1°28'01.55" W]**

Pip's words found in Pip's diary.

No longer in Ana's first floor flat in a Victorian House near the coast of Tynemouth.

Now in 17, Sea View Avenue in Monkseaton.

The diary is spiral bound and the lined sheets of paper are yellow.

The cover has a rainbow stretched across it.

The biro ink is always black.

> > > > >

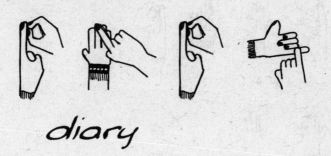

diary

117

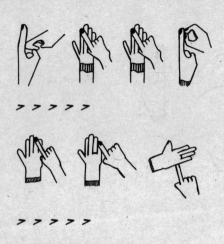

> > > > >

> > > > >

*davie*

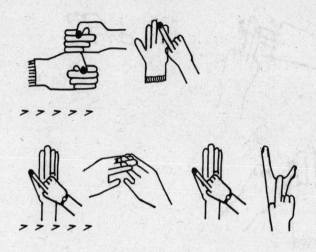

*davie*

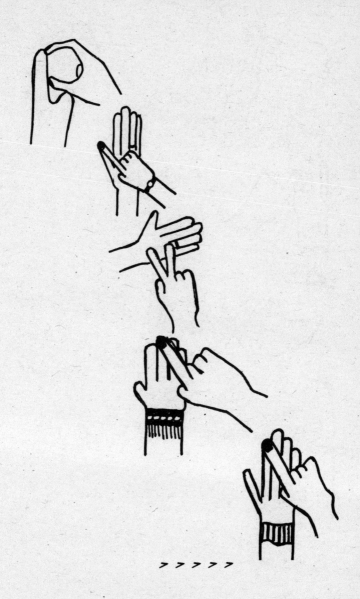

I have two choices. I've got a dog
and my dogs got a lead.
I have the lead in my hand. I can
tie one end of the lead around my
neck. I can attach the other end to
a number of stuff. And then I'll dingle
dangle. I'll dingle dangle like that
scarecrow, in that song that I sang
when I was at playschool. And thats
choice one.
I have another choice though. My
mams been in pain for ages now.
She said she twisted her arm when
she was picking up our Davie. I've
got three months supply of her pain
killers. They arrived two days ago
and she hasnt missed them yet. I've
got them under my bed. I can take
them. I can swallow them all. Theyre
in blistered packets. Waiting for me
to pop pop pop them out. And thats
choice two.

> > > > >

123

Hello.

I was a bit mad the other day.

My names Pip. You know, like a seed.

You see my heart was that shape
when my mam and dad first saw me.
They were looking into my pregnant
mams belly and bits of me were being
pointed out. Then my mam said it
looks like a pip seed. And that was it.
My name kind of stuck.

Ive got to go to school. Ive to go
to school. Ive no choice but to go
to school. I think about bunking off.
I dream about bunking off, but I
cant. My mam would get too mad,
because shed find out. The school
would phone her, then shed get angry.
Shes got too much to deal with. Shes
got her hands full with me and our
Davie and Muppet the dog and dad,
when hes home. (When he decides to
come home.)

Pleased to meet you.

Bye bye.


> > > > >

Hello.

Let me tell you about my dad.

I was seven when my mam shouted up the stairs and told me to come into the kitchen. When I got there my mam was standing washing the dishes in the sink and my dad was sitting on the tiled floor with his back to one of the wooden cupboards and our Davie was crawling around. My mam had shouted in a come now or youll get a smack kind of way. My dad looked sort of funny and his cheeks were bright pink. He was looking at the tiles and speaking really quiet and kind of frog like. My mam turned round from the sink and yelled at him. It was something about him needing to act like a man and find some balls. There were other words. My mam was yelling them out. Anyway, my dad looked up at me. His eyes were all puffy. Were having egg and chips for tea tonight princess, he kind of rushed the words out.

I remember feeling angry that my

Caroline Smailes

mam had shouted me down to tell
me that. But then my mam started
shrieking. Then she just stopped her
yelling at my dad and she looked
straight at me.
Your dads got himself a new family.
He doesnt love us anymore, she spoke
slowly, making sure that each word
was clear. And that was that.
We had our egg and our chips for
tea. We all sat at the kitchen table
eating as normal. Davie was in his
high chair and sucking on his chips.
No one spoke a word, but that was
pretty regular in our house. Mam gave
me more chips than usual and then
when wed all finished my dad left the
table and walked out of the front
door. He didnt pack his bags. Mam
didnt shout and scream anymore.
My dad just left us. Then my mam
cleared the table, scraped the plates
and did the dishes.
But hell come back one day. When hes
had enough of his new missus. Shes
called Sue. But my mam doesnt call

her that. Shes a special word for her.
Its something like frown goathead.
Sues daughter Lucy lives with them
too. Shes thirteen, a year younger
than me and she calls him dad. She
calls my dad dad, but hes not her
dad. And then theres the new bairn.
Sue and my dad had a baby a few
months after he left us. They had
a lad called Kyle. My mam says
that hes only my half brother and
that makes me feel a bit funny. I
love Kyle. I only see him every other
weekend and for an hour or maybe
two. Hes six now and hes funny. Davie
doesnt think so. Davie hates Kyle.
Mam says that she hasnt time to
have a boyfriend and to be getting
herself pregnant. She says that she
hasnt had a good fuck for years. I
havent told her about the stuff I do
with Mike.
Bye bye.


> > > > >

# off Davie and stop
# trying to read this..... /////

Hello.

My mam doesnt like noise in the house.
So me and our Davie decided to
learn about signing stuff. I ripped
a page out of a book in the school
library and me and our Davie have
been learning stuff. Its in our room,
but I made a copy of it in here. It
took me ages. When mams asleep and
our Davie isnt having one of his fits
we use finger signing. Mam gets really
pissed off if we do it in front of her.
She thinks dad taught us it. She
said that dad has a special language
but she wouldnt tell us about it and
I dont really like to ask dad much
stuff.

128

Bye bye.

> > > > >

Hello.
I've had a fuck. I've had several
fucks. I dont really think that I like
it very much.
Bye bye.

> > > > >

Hello.
People say that Im not right. That
Im not right in the head. They think
that Im a fucking nutter. Im a
fucking nutter and a fat ugly cow.
They wrote that I was a fat cow
on the fence. Along the fence that
I have to walk by, in the cut that
runs between number 17 The Coast
Road and the Vets.
I see it on my way home from school.

# Pip is a fat ugly cow.

It's in black paint. It's a special kind

of black paint, the shiny stuff that
they paint on drainpipes that stays
wet so lads cant climb up it and get
into your house or on your roof. And I
think it stains your hands for ever.

# Pip is a fat ugly cow.

Thats me.
Im the only Pip.
Im the only fat ugly cow.
Bye bye.


> > > > >


Hello.
Im fat and ugly.
Bye bye.


> > > > >

> > > > >

Hello.

I live in a place called Tynemouth. Its a bit posh and a bit of a Metro ride away from Newcastle. Tynemouths got a beach and a roller rink and an outdoor swimming pool and loads of really fit surfers. There are loads of huge houses that are really old and some have got really posh people living in them. Anyway theyre really tall and have loads of floors on them. I cant believe that in some of these massive houses theres only one family lives there. Its a bit mad to have one family for all those rooms. Its not like that in our house. We live on the first floor and there are two other flats on this floor. And its not really our house. We rent it from some old bloke who owns the Bonbon sweet shop down the road, but its a nice flat. Well it was a nice flat before mam started to fuck it up. Mam made it nice when we moved in four years ago, but now its all a bit fucked up.

We had to move out of our home,
because my dad couldnt afford to
pay the mortgage anymore. What with
his other family to look after too. So
my life kind of changed. I had to
move to a new school, I had to leave
my mates and I had to share a room
with our Davie. My dad has really
fucked up and I want to hate him,
but I cant. I just wish that hed
come back and fuck my mam again.
Then shed be happy and shed stop
crying when shes in the toilet. And
shed be able to get a job again. Then
wed have some money and Id be able
to get some Nike Air Trainers. Simon
Webb has some at school and I really
need them, but they cost loads of
money and my mam doesnt have any
money. Simon Webb told me that they
feel springy and that they make him
run right fast. I need them. I need
to run fast. I need to run away from
this shitty life.
Bye bye.

> > > > >

Hello.

Our flat has two bedrooms, a living room and the smallest kitchen in the world. I have to share a room with our Davie and hes a pain in the arse most of the time. He messes up my stuff and nicks my pens and paper and he keeps me awake sometimes with his crying in the night. Hes eight now and mam says that hes hard work. Hes always next to her and whenever she comes out and sits down, hes like there with his head on her lap and his legs stretched out over the sofa. I always have to sit on the floor and he looks so fucking smug. Hes got my mam stroking his hair and he gets to be comfy on the only chair weve got. I get to sit on the hard floor and I never get to talk to my mam. Theres loads of stuff that I want to talk to her about. Theres loads of stuff that I need her to help me with. But hes always

there. Our Davies mams favourite.
Davie wets the bed and our room
stinks of his dried up piss. Mam
doesnt realise. I dont think. I cant
remember the last time that she
changed our beds.
Bye bye.


> > > > >


Hello.
The girls who I go with are canny.
Theres Marie and Sarah. Maries my
best friend. But Im not hers. I cant
be hers, because a lass called Donna
told Marie that if she stayed friendly
with me, then shed end up fat and
ugly. Its catching you see. You can
catch being fat and ugly.
I dont know who I caught it off.
Maybe my mam used to be fat and
ugly.
Bye bye.


> > > > >

Hello.

Sarah lives not too far away in a pretty big house. Her dads a solicitor? I think? And her mams a teacher. She gets twelve pound pocket money every week and she spends it on whatever she wants and not clothes and stuff. Her mam buys all her clothes for her from proper shops like Fenwicks in Newcastle.

Bye bye.


> > > > >


Hello.

I went to town with Sarah and Marie. Marie got some really cool bead necklaces from Primark and Sarah got a Justin Timberlake poster. I didnt have any money and I had to nick my metro fare out of our Davies piggy. We had a laugh though. Sarah dared me to lift up my skirt in the middle of Primark. I did it. Sarah and Marie were wetting themselves laughing. Then some dick of a security guard came

and told me to get out the store. He
grabbed my arm and it really hurt.
Then we went back to Sarahs house.
Shes allowed to use drawing pins on
her wall and she put up the Justin
Timberlake poster right above her bed.
Im not allowed to use drawing pins
on my walls because theyre not really
my walls. We rent from the old bloke
who owns the Bonbon sweet shop
and he told mam to tell me that Id
better fucking not mark his walls. Me,
Marie and Sarah were standing on
Sarahs bed looking at the poster on
her wall and the bed collapsed. I felt
really sorry for Sarah. She was crying
her eyes out when her mam came in.
Her mam shouted and told me that I
was too big to be bouncing on beds.
I hadnt been bouncing. I was just
looking at Justin Timberlake. Sarah
and Marie laughed. Marie told Sarahs
mam that I had been bouncing. Shes
a lying cow.
Bye bye.

> > > > >

Hello.
I didnt tell mam about Sarahs bed.
I should have done, because when
I was in bed Sarahs mam phoned.
I heard my mam crying down the
phone. She was saying sorry and that
she couldnt stop me from eating. Im
really angry with my mam for telling
Sarahs mam crap like that. I know
what Sarahs like. Shell tell everyone
at school that Im a fat greedy pig
who cant stop eating.
They all think it anyway.
Bye bye.

> > > > >

Hello.
I dont know how to stop eating so
its not really surprising that Im a
fat greedy ugly cow pig.
Bye bye.

> > > > >

Hello.

<u>School</u>

# Pip is a fat ugly cow.

It's still on the fence.

In the cut.

Along the cut.

It's still there in huge letters all the way along. I see it out of the corner of my eye. As I walk home from school all the other kids see it too, they look at it though and they laugh at it. They think that its fucking funny. I dont think that its fucking funny. I cant get rid of it.

I dont know how to get rid of it. I cant figure out what to do. Its on someones fence and if I get caught scribbling out on someones fence well I'll get into loads of trouble. They'll tell my mam and shell get mad and shes already got too much to deal with.

I dont want to make her sad.

I want her to stop crying.

I need her to stop crying.

I can hear her you see. The door

muffles, but it doesnt stop the sound
of my mams sobbing.
I want to make my mam happy again
so that she can start being a real
mam again.
Bye bye.


> > > > >


Hello.
Davie finger signed to me to fuck off.
He spelt fuc without a k. I laughed
at him and he started screaming.
Mam didnt wake up. She had taken
one of her pills.
Bye bye.


> > > > >

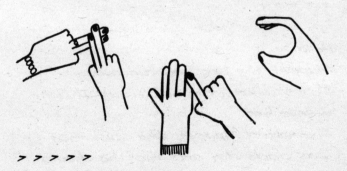

> > > > >

Hello.

<u>School.</u>

We finished school at 2.25pm,
because of the snow. I hate the
fucking snow. I was coming home from
school and Jake jumped on me. I was
on the floor and he scrubbed me. He
got it down my top. He put his hand
down my top and had a right grope
of my tits. Hes a dirty bastard, but
I quite like him. I might ask him out
tomorrow.

I was supposed to be going sledging
down Tynemouth golf course with
Marie and Sarah. But they didnt
come for me.

Bye bye.


> > > > >


Hello.

Muppet the dog has run away.
Thats what mam said, but I dont
believe her.

She hated Muppet. She said that he
was dads dog and that he should

fucking pay for him, but that doesnt matter anymore, because Muppets not here and neither are his toys and his basket. Our Davies really worried about Muppet.

Bye bye.

> > > > >

Hello.

### School

I fancy a lad called Dobson. I think that I do anyway.

I dont really really though, because really I like Mike.

Mike is the lad who I fuck.

Hes in my year, but not in my form.

He doesnt speak to me at school, but I meet him when its dark and I do loads of stuff with him. Like sometimes he fucks me and I sometimes suck his cock and I sometimes wank him off.

No one knows about it at school because I think were secret lovers like that right old Atlantic Star song

that mam used to play, but he says
that he doesnt want anyone to know
because Im a fat ugly cow.
Bye bye.


> > > > >


Hello.
_School_
I had the first practice for
Oklahoma today. Were doing it at
school and Im in the chorus. Marie
and Sarah are too. They didnt want
to dance with me and the dance
had to be two girls, so I dont have
a partner. I sit at the back with
a parasol, while the people with
partners dance on the front of the
stage. They get to dance and spin
and stuff with their parasols and I
get to sit on a pile of hay right at
the back. Its shitty crap.
Our Davie drew five pictures of
Muppet and stuck them onto five
pieces of card with MISSING in
capitals at the top and our address

and phone number on the bottom. I helped him with the spelling and the phone number. Mam said that he cant stick them onto lampposts. She said that he couldnt because hed put our address and phone number on them and every fucking weirdo would be calling her up and she didnt want every fucking weirdo to phone her up. She threw our Davies posters in the bin. Then she was all calm and she opened a tin of Coop baked beans and poured them into the bin, over the paper. Our Davie was jumping up and down screaming and his hands were flying all over the place. Mam turned and threw the empty tin of Coop baked beans at our Davie and it hit him smack on his face. She said that he had no right to scream at her and that he was getting more like dad everyday.

Davies still crying now.

And I dont know how to make him better. He does look like dad, but I kind of think that he doesnt look like

dad too. Hes got really blonde hair
and his eyes are exactly the same
blue like dad. Kyle has the eyes too,
but hes got dark brown hair like Sue.
Bye bye.


> > > > >


Hello.
Mams in her bed and Davies still
crying. I feel kind of bad because
I helped him to write our address
and phone number onto the posters. I
know that our Davie misses Muppet
the dog.
I wish dad would phone. I finger
signed to Davie love and he finger
signed back fuc. I laughed.
Bye bye.


> > > > >

> > > > >

> > > > >

Hello.

## School

School was really shit today. Terry
brought in a photograph of a really
really fat woman that he had found
in his mams magazine. He said she was
my twin sister.

I dont have a twin sister and the
fat woman was really old and stuff.
Terry Kept on walking in front of me
and shoving the fat woman in my
face. Him and Dobson were following
me around everywhere. I got sent
home from school with a headache.
Mam was in bed, so I made myself a
fish finger and tomato sauce toasted
sandwich and sat in my room. Davie
hadnt gone to school. He wet himself

before he even left the house and he
didnt have any clean clothes. He was
still wearing his stinking pants when
I came home from school and he was
just lying on the sofa like a fucking
freak. I made him a fish finger and
tomato sauce toasted sandwich too.
Im dreading school on Monday.
Bye bye.


> > > > >


Hello.
_School_
I went back to school. Terry was
off, but Dobson asked if I was
pregnant. I said no and he said that
hed give me a fuck if I wanted. I
think that he was joking, because he
laughed afterwards. I think I kind
of fancy him, but I dont know if
he likes me. I think I should let him
fuck me a bit.
Bye bye.


> > > > >

Hello,

I met Mike in Tynemouth Primary
playground at 9 oclock. Mam had
taken some of her pills and was
asleep and our Davie was in bed. I
took my key and I locked them in.
Mike said that he wanted to fuck
Gemma Lyle, but that she was a
frigid cow. He said that he liked me
because I was a good fuck. I let
him lick my fanny. He said that I
tasted funny. I asked him what I
tasted like. He said for me to try.
He put two fingers in me and then I
licked them. Mike said that I was a
dirty bitch. Then he put on one of his
brothers condoms and he fucked me.
Afterwards he hung the condom on
the door handle into the school. He
didnt walk me home, because he
didnt want anyone to see him with
me. I wanted to walk home with
him. I wanted him to hold my hand.
I asked him to. He said that he
wouldnt be seen dead walking along
the road holding my hand. He said

that my hand and my fingers were dirty. Then he ran off and shouted dirty bitch.
Bye bye.

> > > > >

Hello.
I think I am a dirty bitch.
I came home and stuck my fingers in me and then I licked them again. I think I do taste funny and now my face really stinks and we dont have any soap.
Bye bye.

> > > > >

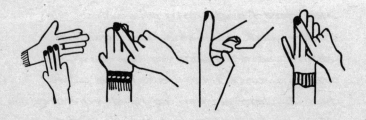

> > > > >

Hello.

Mam thinks shes Rapunzel. I think theres something really wrong with her head. She keeps shouting out Rapunzel Rapunzel let down your hair. I think shes off her head. Davie heard her too and he started doing a fake laugh. Then it went into a real laugh and he wet himself again. He fucking stinks.

Bye bye.

> > > > >

Hello.

<u>School</u>

It was the school disco tonight from 6 oclock till 8. There was a tuck-shop and Mr Penns was in charge. Sarah said that he was a filthy perve and kept looking down her top and she said that he pushed some girl who left a few years ago into a cupboard and tried to rape her. Hes such a filthy perve.

I dont have many clothes that fit

anymore. Mam said that it'd be nice
if I wore her suit that she used to
wear when she worked. Mam used
to work in an office. She used to sell
stuff over the phone and she'd get
loads of really cool freebie stuff. She
got a twenty pound voucher once for
Woolworths. She hasn't worked for
two years and she doesn't really go
out much. She just slobs around in
her trackie bottoms and baggy t-
shirts. She makes the flat stink a
bit and I have to keep telling her to
have a bath. She shouts at me if I
tell her to do anything like that.
I wore her old pink suit for the disco.
It fit which is a bit fucked because
my mam is supposed to be bigger than
me. I think that I'm really fat. The
skirt was pleated and the jacket
was really posh with shiny buttons
on it. Dobson said that I looked a
state and Mike just stared at me.
He kept giving me the shitty looks. I
was really hot and sweaty, but I
didn't want to take the jacket off,

because the white silky blouse had a huge iron burn mark on the back.

I'm really crap at ironing. Mam says that I'm too easily distracted, but I was trying to iron and make our Davies tea and I only had an hour before the disco started and I left the iron on my mams favourite work shirt. I dont understand why she got so shouty for, its not like shes ever going to wear it again.

Nearly all the songs at the disco were love ones. And Mike was dancing with Gemma Lyle for all of them. He snogged her and put his hand on her arse. I spent most of the night crying in the cloakroom.

I walked home from the disco on my own. Mam was in bed and our Davie was falling asleep on the sofa. I told him to fuck off to bed but he just started crying instead. He said that I should fuck off to bed and then he got on his stomach and bawled. I asked him what had happened and he told me to fuck off.

Mike phoned and told me to meet him at Tynemouth Primary playground at 9 oclock. I checked on mam but shed taken one of her pills and was asleep on top of her bed. I told our Davie that Id be back in a bit and he ignored me. Hes a fucking idiot.
I took my key and I locked Davie in. Mike said that he wanted to fuck Gemma Lyle, but that she was a frigid cow. She was a cock tease and wouldnt let him poke her or anything. He said that he liked me because I was a dirty bitch and a good fuck. He put on one of his brothers condoms and he fucked me. I was home by half past 9 and our Davie was still crying.
Bye bye.


> > > > >


Hello.
Sometimes I wish that my mam would be a proper mam and shed get dressed in nice clothes and do

her hair and put on mascara or
something. She keeps saying mad
stuff about being trapped in her red
room, but theres a door and stuff.
Shes doing my head in. I just want
to go shopping with my mam and do
normal stuff like Sarah and Marie do
with their mams. My mams so fucked
up and my dads not making it any
better.
Bye bye.


> > > > >


Hello.
Our Davie asked me what it meant
that I fucked Mike. I think he has
been reading this. Fuck off Davie. Go
wet yourself again.
Bye bye.


> > > > >

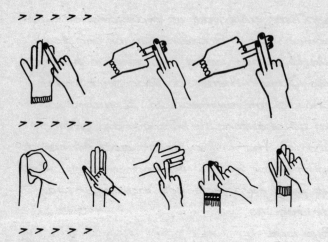

Hello.

<u>School</u>

It was my grandma in Bykers
birthday today. My dad came after
hed finished work to pick us up. When
we got to my grandma in Bykers
house Sue was already there. Her
and Lucy and Kyle had already had
their tea because there wasnt enough
chairs for us all to sit round the
table. My grandma in Byker had made
some coconut stacks, but Kyle had
nicked all the cherries off the top.
Our Davie was really pissed off and

154

told our grandma in Byker that Kyle was a cunt. Grandma in Byker gave our Davie a wallop on his ear and our Davie screamed. Dad took him outside and sorted him out, but when he came back he sat on the chair next to the fire and refused to eat anything.

It was really depressing. Lucy was all laughing with my grandma and Sue was talking about Lucys dancing show. I hate Lucy. Shes so fucking perfect and everything she wears matches. Shes like this fucking perfect princess and everyone worships her. Dad had forgotten to put mine and Davies name on my grandma in Bykers birthday card and I didnt have a present for her. It was dead embarrassing and I think that my grandma was really pissed off with me and Davie. She didnt give us any pocket money when we left. I dont think she gave fucking perfect Lucy any either. I asked my grandma in Byker if I could take some coconut

stacks home for me and Davie. She
said that I couldnt because she
wanted to take them to bingo with
her. I really do think that shes right
pissed off with me and Davie.
Dad dropped us outside the flat.
I went in with our Davie and mam
shouted at us. She was in the bath
with her clothes on. She had drank
half a bottle of Martini and she was
holding a packet of her tablets. She
said that if we left her again she
was going to take the tablets and
then wed have to go and live in a
kiddies home because no one else loved
us. Our Davie started screaming and
then he wet himself. My mam didnt
even notice. She was too busy sobbing.
I had to shut up our Davie and then
I had to wait for mam to puke from
the Martini. She puked everywhere and
dropped the tablets. I nicked them
and put them under my bed in my
room. Our Davie stood watching the
whole thing. His pants were fucking
soaking and he stank of piss.

This is all my fucking dads fault for
making us go to my grandma in Bykers
house. My dad just keeps on fucking
up and I want to hate him and I
am trying to, but I cant really hate
him. I know my mam wants me to
hate my dad and that shes really
pissed off we still want to see him,
but I love my dad. I know that if
he came back and fucked my mam
again, then shed feel better.
And shed stop doing all the mad
stuff. I really want her to stop with
all the fucking mad stuff.
Bye bye.


> > > > >


Hello.
Grandma in Byker isnt really my
grandma. Shes my dads dads missus.
I dont know where my dads dad
is and I dont know where my dads
mam is. I havent ever met my dads
mam before. My mam says that she
is an evil bitch who wanted to kill me

when I was in my mams tummy. She says that my dads mam dragged her to the hospital to have me sucked out of her, but my mam escaped. I think my dads mam hates me and our Davie, but Lucy and Kyle have met her. Lucy says that she is proper rich and has false nails. All I know is that my family is really fucked up.
Bye bye.

> > > > >

Hello.
Davie I know youre still reading this.

# Fuck off....... ////////

Bye bye.

> > > > >

> > > > >

> > > > >

Hello.

Were not supposed to make any noise
when mams asleep. The problem is
that mam is always fucking asleep.
She takes loads of tablets and when
they knock her out Davie and me are
not supposed to make any noise. So
me and Davie lie in our beds and try
to spell things out with finger signing.
It takes ages to say one word and
our Davie is really crap at spelling.
Sometimes I really hate it when there
isnt any noise because then when our
Davie starts crying it really makes my
head hurt.

Bye bye.


> > > > >


Hello.

I dont let mam see me cry and I

dont let our Davie see me cry. I can cry without making any noise. I cry loads and no one notices. I think Im a bit fucked up.
Bye bye.

> > > > >

Hello.
I found out that my mam had walked to the offy in her dirty trackie, no shoes and a really old t-shirt that used to be my dads. Sarah and her mam had drove past her.
I am so fucking ashamed.
Bye bye.

> > > > >

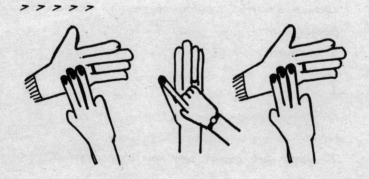

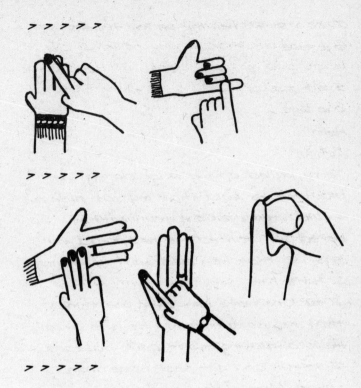

> > > > >

Hello.

_School_

I asked out Johna and Dobson
today. No luck. I only did it because
we were in science and Mike sits next
to them. Mike just laughed and said
that he didn't know anyone whod
want to go out with a fat ugly cow.

I can still smell me on my fingers.
Bye bye.

> > > > >

Hello.

<u>School</u>

Terry pulled up my skirt during wet
playtime. He said that my fat arse
would stop everyone from getting
bored. He wanted me to spread my
legs, so that he could sniff my fanny.
I hate him.
I fucking hate him. Everyone thinks
that hes so funny and he isnt at all.
He is a fucking twat cunt bastard.
I felt ill and got sent home from
school. Mam didnt mind because she
was having one of her bad days.
She told me to get our Davie from
school and when he saw me our Davie
started bawling. He asked me if our
mam was dead. I said no but he
didnt believe me and he ran all the
way to the flat like a screaming
freakoid.

Bye bye.

> > > > >

Hello.

## No school

I didnt want to go to school today.
I felt ill and not right. Mam said
that she likes it when Im off. I
hoovered and dusted and sorted
out the washing for mam to do. She
doesnt like doing the washing and I
keep having to get knickers out of the
dirty washing tub. I was going to
do the washing but I couldnt find
any powder stuff. Mam said to use
washing up liquid, but I dont even
know if we have any washing up stuff
left. Mam needs to do a big shop
when she gets her social.
Sarah gave a me depressing phone
call. Im not doing the waltz with
her in Oklahoma either because I
was sent home yesterday and she
chose Marie to be her partner in the
rehearsals today. That means that ill

be stuck at the back again like the
parasol one and watching everyone
else dancing and stuff.
Bye bye.

> > > > >

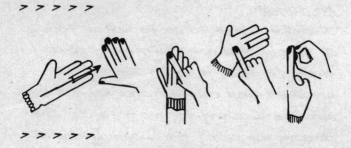

> > > > >

Hello.
Mam asked me to come in her room.
I went in and she told me the story
about how I got my name and about
the pip shape on the screen. I've
heard that story loads of times but
I still like it. Mam tells it and then
she starts crying. She says that it all
went a bit fucked after that. Mam
says that everything will be alright
if me and Davie can make our dad
love us again. Mam says that then
our dad will come home and fuck her

again and that she hasnt had a good
fuck for ages. Then she laughs and
its all a bit mad. Mam just lies on
her bed and stares out through her
window. She can see the coast and
the fit surfers. Her room stinks and
the red wallpaper is peeling off. I
wish my mam would change her bed
and hoover around her room a bit. If
my dad comes back hes going to think
shes mad.
Bye bye.

> > > > >

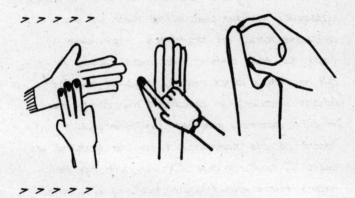

> > > > >

Hello.
Marie phoned up and said that she
wanted to do the waltz with me

because Sarah was a two-faced cow and had been slagging me off. I asked Marie what Sarah had been saying but she didnt want to say. Sarah is such a bitch and I hate her.

Dad was supposed to be picking us up and taking us to our grandma in Bykers house. Our Davie got up when it was still dark and he was dressed and everything. He does a really stupid laugh whenever dads supposed to be coming to see us. Its a stupid squeaky giggle because hes so excited and he kind of patters from one foot to the other. He was doing it all morning and really pissing me off. Mam stayed in bed all morning, but thats pretty normal on the days that dads supposed to be taking us out. I asked our Davie not to tell mam that dad was taking us to grandma in Bykers house, so we just told her that dad was taking us to McDonalds and that we wished we were staying with her.

I used to think that she stayed
in bed on the mornings dad was
coming so that dad would go into the
bedroom and get into bed with her.
Then he could fuck her sadness and
stuff out of her.
But I dont think that anymore,
because she stinks and her room
stinks the same. I dont think that
she washes her fanny and I really
wish that she would.
Anyway, my dad still wasnt there
at ten past twelve and our Davie
started screaming and ripping up
stuff. He ripped up this dead nice
book that dad had given me when I
was little. So I slapped our Davie
across his face and told him to fuck
off. Davie started screaming for mam
but she didnt do anything.
I phoned dad to see where he was,
but he wasnt there and no one was
there, so I thought that maybe he
was on his way. I told our Davie
that dad would be here soon and our
Davie cheered up a bit. He even went

into mams room and sat on her bed
looking out the window with mam,
but dad didnt come and he didnt
phone to say that he wasnt coming
and our Davie has put stuff behind
our bedroom door. Mam said that
dad was a twat, but she wouldnt
get out of bed to help me.
I cant get the door open and I dont
Know what to do.
I cant make everything better.
I dont fucking Know what to do.
Bye bye.

> > > > >

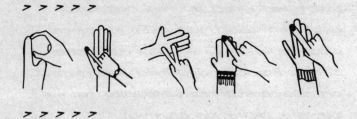

> > > > >

Hello.
Mike phoned.
He wanted to Know if I could get
out again.
So I waited till Davie stopped crying

and mam was asleep and I went
to meet Mike in Tynemouth Primary
playground. Mike had already started
wanking himself off. He was hard and
stuff had started to dribble. He told
me to get on the floor and spread
my legs. He didnt even take off my
Knickers. He pushed them to the
side and then he fucked me. I had
only just got there. He didnt bring
a condom, because his brother had
started hiding them. Then he told me
that he better not catch something
from me. He said that I was a dirty
bitch and that I stunk. He said
that hed have to wash his dick in
bleach. Then he went.
I stood up and his stuff started
pouring out. It was dripping down
my leg when I walked home. Id only
been out for half an hour and when
I got home there was fucking chaos.
Our Davie had stopped calming down
and decided to phone dad. Hed
thought dad was dead. Anyway dad
told our Davie that he hadnt come

today because Lucy had been in a
gymnastics competition and that hed
phoned mam and told her to tell us.
Our Davie had called him a fucking
liar and then pulled the phone out of
the socket. Then he trashed everything
and I got home as he was trashing
everything.
And I couldnt stop him, because hes
got really strong and stuff.
Mam had taken one of her pills that
she takes to help her sleep.
I fucking hate my dad.
Bye bye.


> > > > >


Hello.
I wish that my mam would read my
diary.
Bye bye.


> > > > >


Hello.
Back to school.

The history exam was rock.
I've done really bad. Terry wrote
RIP on the back of my shirt in black
biro that doesn't wash out. Mam is
going to freak when she sees it. I
don't know if I should hide it in the
washing or throw it away.
The freezer is full of food again. Mam
spent her social on loads of stuff.
Bye bye.

> > > > >

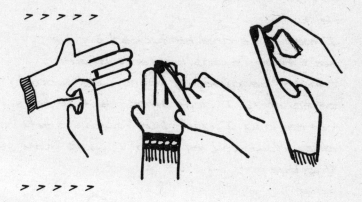

> > > > >

Hello.
Went to town with our Davie and our
grandma in Byker. We went into the
pound shop and the butchers. It was
dead boring. We went back and had

fish and chips. Then dad came and took us back to mam. Our grandma in Byker gave me and Davie fifty pence each. I told our Davie that Id look after his for him and that he wasnt to tell mam that wed been to grandma in Bykers.
Bye bye.

> > > > >

Hello.
I met Mike and he fucked me. He said that it was better without a condom because my fanny was warm on his dick. I dont think that it feels better and I dont like how his stuff drips down my leg when I walk home.
Bye bye.

> > > > >

172

> > > > >

Hello.
Davie fuck off reading my diary.
If you tell mam about Mike I'm
going to kill you.

You are so pissing me
off Davie..... /////

Bye bye.

> > > > >

Hello.
Mam asked me if she was a bad
mam. I said no. I dont think that
shes bad I just think that shes
fucked up since dad left. Mam
asked if I wanted to live with dad
and Sue instead of her. I said no,
but sometimes I wish that we did
because Sue takes Lucy out shopping
for clothes and stuff from Primark.
I think that Sue is a good mam

to Lucy. Lucy is always happy and
she does loads of hobbies and stuff
and she is so pretty. I think my
dad wishes that she was his real
daughter.
I need to hate my dad and love my
mam a bit more.
Bye bye.

> > > > >

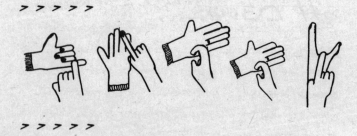

> > > > >

Hello.
Sarah phoned. She is devastated
because theyre closing Primark in
Newcastle. Sarah doesnt know where
she will get her clothes from anymore.
I wanted to tell her to fuck off but
I didnt. I wish my mam would read
this and take me shopping to Primark
before it closes down. I think that

if I had proper clothes then I might
feel happy.
Bye bye.

> > > > >

Hello.
_School_
I lost my coat, but then I found
a pair of trainers. They looked like
Emma Cooks. I took them into her
science room and straight away Terry
took the mick. He shouted out that
the floor was breaking and that I
was going to cause an earthquake.
Everyone laughed. I was so
embarrassed I nearly died. I went
to the toilets and cried.
I got sent home from school for having
a headache and stuff. Mam was
asleep because I think shed taken
one of her pills. I made 10 fish fingers
and put them in toasted sandwiches
with loads of tomato sauce. I felt a
bit sick after.
Bye bye.

> > > > >

Hello.
Sarah told me that last night Johna
and Terry said they were going to
rape me, but Johna or Terry said I
was too tight.
I asked Johna and Terry which one
said it and they each said it was
the other one. Johna says that Terry
is a stirrer. I hate Terry, but I
fancy Johna a bit. I am not going to
ask him out.
Bye bye.

> > > > >

Hello.
I fancy Mike, Johna, Terry, Dobson,
Keith, Stevo and Gemma Lyles
brother. Ive fucked Mike 28 times.
Bye bye.

> > > > >

Hello.

Today was fine until this afternoon.
After form I started down the stairs
and Terry pushed me. I think my foot
missed the step, because I went
flying down the stairs and banged
my head on the bottom door. I have
never ever been in such pain and my
skirt went right up and everyone
could see my scanky knickers. I think
I was knocked out a bit but I dont
know because I remember hearing
everyone laughing and wondering why
no one was helping me.

I got taken home by Olga the
secretary woman, but mam wasnt
opening the door. Olga had to take
me to hospital and pretend to be my
mam. I had nine x-rays but nothing
was broken. The nurse put a bandage
on my arm and told me that I had
to wear a sling. I think that my fat
must have protected my bones.

Sarah phoned and said that Terry
had been laughing about it all day
at school. He had been telling everyone

that hed hurt his back pushing me.
Sarah said that Terry had been
limping around school, bending over like
he was an old man. Sarah said that
Terry was really funny.
Sarah asked me why I wore such
tatty knickers.
Im dreading going back to school.
Terrys going to be even more horrible
to me and I didnt snitch on him or
anything because I said that I fell,
but I didnt fall at all and it really
hurt.
Lucky Im so fat otherwise I might
have died.
Bye bye.

> > > > >

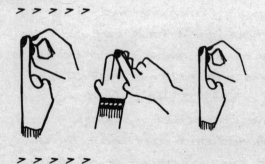

> > > > >

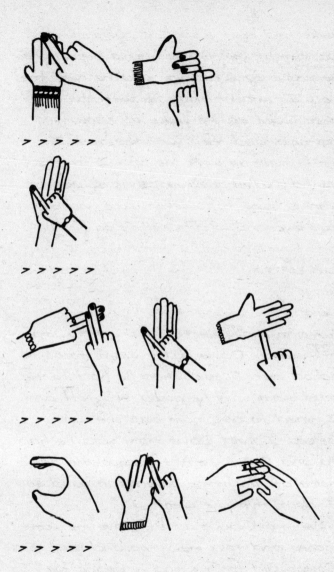

Hello.

Last night our Davie had a nightmare.
He woke up screaming and he wet the
bed. It wasnt that he wet the bed
then woke up. He woke up screaming
for ages and then wet the bed. I
let him get in with me and I stroked
his hair a bit. He was shaking and he
stinks.

Bye bye.

> > > > >

Hello.

My arm really hurts so I got to stay
off school, Davie didnt want to go to
school but I said that he had to. He
said mam said he could stay off and
I tried to ask mam but she was
asleep. I told Davie mam said he had
to and Davie went to school. He came
home at lunchtime covered in sand so
I dont think he went.

When mam woke up she gave me some
money and told me to go and buy
Cosmo Girl for me and a Beano for

our Davie. She couldnt really afford
to and I think that she took the
money out of our Davies piggy, but it
was really canny of her. Davie came
with me to the shops. He seemed a
bit happy and kept finger signing
Beano all the way.
Bye bye.

> > > > >

> > > > >

Hello.
I phoned Marie to find out what had
been said about me and to tell her
how sore my arm was. The bandage
gets on my wick and I cant do
anything. Marie said that nothing was
said at school, but I could tell that
she was lying. She was being different
with me.
Bye bye.

> > > > >

Hello.
I phoned Marie to ask her why
she was being different. She said
that she wasnt sure she could be
my friend anymore. She said I was
getting a bit too fat.
I dont even want to be friends with
a stuck up tight bitch.
Bye bye.

> > > > >

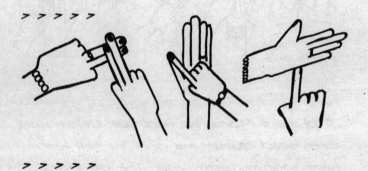

> > > > >

Hello.
I took two of mams pills. I was
going to take more but I was a bit
scared. Our Davie was watching me
I think. Everything is so fucked up.

182

I wish my mam would wake up a bit more and be my best friend. Marie and Sarah say their mams are like proper friends. My mam doesn't really talk to me about stuff that happens now. She just keeps telling me not to blink and it's kind of doing my head in. What the fuck does don't blink mean? Bye bye.

> > > > >

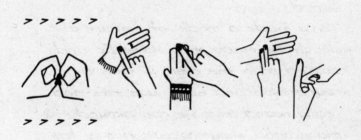

> > > > >

Hello.
Mam gave me a disposable razor and told me not to cut me or our Davie with it. I don't know if that means she wants me to or not.
Bye bye.

> > > > >

Hello.
Mike phoned and said that he had

shagged Gemma Lyle and that she
was a better fuck than me. Mike
said that she didnt stink and that
her tits were lush.
Bye bye.

> > > > >

Hello.
<u>School</u>
Terry made a model of me out of
dough. He made it in Home Ec and
cooked it in the oven. I was a
round blob and had huge tits and
really round legs. He ran around the
playground shouting out this is fat
Pip. This is fat Pip.
I am fat Pip.
I am fat Pip.
I am fucking fat Pip.....//////
I went to the medical room. I felt
sick. I was sent home.
Mam likes it when Im sent home and
Davie is starting to not run home
thinking mam is dead when I go and
pick him up.

Bye bye.

> > > > >

Hello.
Davie keeps doing finger signing for
cut. I think he wants me to cut
him but I dont want to. I dont like
blood and I dont want to hurt our
Davie.
Bye bye.

> > > > >

> > > > >

Hello.
Mike phoned.
He wanted to know if I could get
out again. I waited till our Davie
was in bed and I went to meet Mike

185

in Tynemouth Primary playground. Mike
had his dick out. He was gripping
it. He told me to get on the floor
and spread my legs. I didnt have
any knickers on, because I didnt
have any clean ones. Mike said I
was a dirty bitch wanting a fuck.
Mike fucked me. He hadnt brought
a condom, because his brother had
ran out. He said that I was a dirty
bitch and that I stunk. He said that
he was thinking about Gemma Lyle
when he fucked me and then he went.
I didnt stand up. I didnt want his
stuff to pour out of me.
Bye bye.


> > > > >


Hello.
I dont think I like being me. Its so
fucked up. I wish my mam would
make it better but she keeps taking
her pills and its like shes not even
here. I havent spoken to her for three
days now.

Bye bye.

> > > > >

Hello.

Our Davie stinks and its really bad. He squeezes his dick instead of going to the toilet. He says that it hurts when he pees. He waits too long and then he pisses himself.

Mam doesnt care and dad hasnt been for ages. Im the only one who cares and our Davie is getting really clingy. He keeps getting in my bed in the night. Im worried hell wet my bed too and mam will think it was me.

I wish mam would come in our room and smell how bad it is. She never comes in. Shes going out less and less now. I have to do the shopping and get her social from the post office now too, but at least I get to stay off school on a Tuesday.

Bye bye.

> > > > >

Hello.

Me and our Davie sat on my bed
with that disposable razor again.
Davie kept finger signing cut but I
dont know how you cut with it. I
can cut my fingers but it kind of
just makes little scratches. Davie
was getting all excited he kept finger
signing.

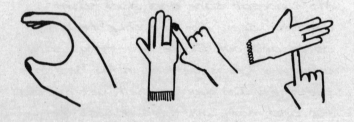

But I couldnt make it cut properly
and I dont think I like blood
anyway. Our Davie took the razor and
made a scratch on top of his finger
and then he started picking it. I
watched him. He made it bleed loads
on my bed. He showed me his leg. He
picks there too and there are loads
of scabby things that are really gross

and theres loads of blood in his finger
nails. I think he likes doing it.
I went and made us loads of fish
fingers for tea and he didnt wash his
hands before he ate them.
Bye bye.


> > > > >


Hello.
I love our Davie even if he is
fucked up.
Bye bye.


> > > > >

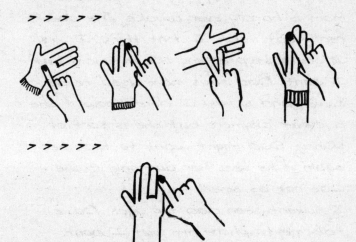


> > > > >

189

> > > > >

> > > > >

Hello.

Im a fat and ugly cow but I cant
stop eating. I am so hungry and I
like food. I bought some mint cakes
and stuff for the freezer because
I do all the shopping now because
mam is hardly ever awake. She doesnt
really eat much I dont think. I wish
I could stop eating like my mam but
I cant. Dad says mam used to be
clever and skinny. I dont know if she
is clever anymore but she is sort of
skinny. Dad might want to fuck her
again if he sees her but only if she
was not as smelly.

I havent seen dad for ages. Davie
tells me to phone him but I dont
want to because me and Davie look

a state. Mam hasnt done any washing for ages and she wont tell me how to do it. I keep trying to wash stuff in the sink but I cant do it right and everything keeps getting really hard. Bye bye.

> > > > >

Hello.

Weve got no heating and no phone now. Its all so fucked up. Davie and me just sit together and I try to make him finger sign words because that stops him picking his scabby fingers. They have stuff coming from them thats not blood. Bye bye.

> > > > >

Hello.

<u>School day but no school.</u>

Im at dad and Sues house.

He took us with him last night. Id been out fucking Mike and I didnt

lock our Davie in because he is ok
with me going out for a little bit. I
told him I was going to buy some
sweets. When I came back our Davie
was trashing the flat again and mam
wasnt waking up.
I didnt know what to do and then
our Davie told me that hed gone
to the phone box and phoned dad.
Davie was all screamy. He said dad
didnt love us anymore and mam never
woke up. Davie was going mad and
I didnt know what to do. I still
had Mikes stuff dripping down my
leg. I was wearing mams old trackie
bottoms because none of my stuff
fits anymore.
Im a fat cow.. //
Dad came around and he saw
the flat really trashed. Davie had
stopped breaking and ripping stuff
and was sitting on the floor picking
at his fingers. I was sitting next to
him and the door was open because
Davie had tried to pull it down. It
was kind of bent off. Our Davie is

right strong now.

Dad saw that our Davie had shit
and pissed himself and he asked
where mam was. Davie told him that
mam hadnt woken up. Dad had a
look around the kitchen and the
bathroom and our room. They were
dirty, because I cant keep up with
the cleaning. Theres too much to do
and dad was shouting and saying
shit and bollocks and fucking hell
and loads of stuff like that. I didnt
know my dad swore. Dad spent ages
in mine and Davies room. He asked me
why I had all mams tablets in my
room. I told him that I looked after
them for mam. I think he called mam
a lazy cunt, but I dont know. He
was swearing loads. I thought that
dad was having a go at me and I
started crying. Then he gave me a hug
and said that I was still a bairn
and that I shouldnt have to hear all
this grown up shit.

I told him that if he came back and
fucked mam, then everything would be

alright. He didnt say anything for ages after that and I thought he was going to tell me that he didnt like me. Then he told us to pack a bag. I said that we didnt have any clean stuff and he didnt shout at me.
He said not to bother and then told us to go and get in the car while he had a word with mam.
I told him that there was no point and that she wouldnt wake up when shed taken one of her pills.
Dad told us to get our school stuff and to get in the car and we did.
Today Davie and me are off school, but Lucy and Kyle had to go to school. Sue got us some new clothes to wear from a proper shop and made us have baths and stuff.
I havent spoken to mam yet.
Bye bye.

> > > > >

Hello.
School, but no school

Sue and dad took our Davie to our grandma in Bykers house and me to a doctor today, but dad didnt come in with us. He stayed in the waiting room reading a magazine about geography or something. I dont think that he was really reading it.

The doctor asked me loads of questions. She asked about my mam and about school and about friends. She was canny nice. Then she asked me if I had a boyfriend and I didnt want to talk about Mike because Mike had told me not to, so I kept my mouth shut and she kept on talking.

She started talking about sex and condoms and loads of embarrassing stuff like that. I didnt really know what she was telling me. I didnt tell her that I knew about that kind of stuff. Then she said that she wanted to examine me and that I had to lie on the table thing and so I did. She examined my big fat tummy and I was waiting for her to tell me that

I was a fat ugly cow. She prodded
and poked around a bit and it hurt
when she did it hard.
Then I had to go and pee in a little
bottle and I pissed most of it onto
my fingers. Then she dipped a stick
of paper into my pee and then put it
flat on her desk.
She kept talking to me, but her eyes
kept flicking onto the piss covered
paper and I really didn't have a clue
what she was doing. Then she told
me to go and tell my dad to come in
and I did. Sue told me not to worry
and I think shes kind of canny really.
I wasn't worried. I got dad and he
looked all puffy and red and stressy
and then we all sat down.
And then the doctor told me that
I was pregnant and she asked if I
knew what that meant and I said
yes.
I still havent spoken to mam.
Bye bye.

> > > > >

# Black Boxes

> > > > >

Hello,

<u>School, but no school</u>

I havent spoken to Marie or Sarah
and I dont even know if dad has
phoned the school. I bet that Im
not doing the line dance in Oklahoma.
Marie and Sarah will be doing it
together and I'll be stuck at the
back again. Lucy and Kyle are
sleeping at Sues mams for a few days
and our Davie wants to go too. He
has decided that he likes Kyle and
Kyle is letting him play with his toys
and stuff.

Our Davie hasnt cried since we got
here and he hasnt asked about mam.
Sue has put plasters on his fingers
to help him and she says she is going
to find him a lady to talk to. I dont
really understand whats going on but
it is warm and clean in dad and sues
house and they have Sky TV. Davie
told me last night that Kyle was his
brother. I dont want Lucy to be my

sister. Shes a stuck up bitch and she looks down on me because Im not pretty and skinny like her. The house is too small for all of us. Its got three bedrooms and one of them is really small. So I know that we cant stay here. There isnt enough room, so well have to go home soon.

I want to know if mams alright, but Im too scared to ask dad.

Sue keeps coming in to the room. Shes right nosey and keeps asking me loads of questions and shes like so annoying, but she keeps making me drinks and stuff and I havent had to do any dishes or stuff since Ive been here. She bought me the nicest pair of Levi jeans and they fit me and theyve not been worn by anyone but me. I wish that I didnt like her, but she is being canny to me.

Mam is going to be so pissed with me. My dad has been out all day today. I dont think that he went to work, because he wasnt wearing work clothes when he left. And I dont

think that hell be fucking mam,
because I think that him and Sue
are happy fucking each other.
I miss my mam.
Bye bye.


> > > > >


Hello.
<u>School, but no school</u>
Im pregnant.
Do I know what that means.? No.
I dont know what that means.
And no one is talking about it so its
bound to go away.
How am I pregnant.? Im still at
school and you can only get pregnant
when youre old and in your 20's
or something like that. I think the
doctor made a mistake.
Bye bye.


> > > > >


Hello.
Dad told me that Mams in hospital.

Shes sick.

Dad says that shes too sick for us to visit her.

I dont know if its catching because dad hasnt told us what is actually wrong with mam, but she is too sick to speak to us and too sick for us to visit so I think she is really really sick.

I asked dad if mam was going to die and he said that he didnt want to talk about it but I wasnt to tell Davie about mam dying. I dont understand whats going on. Dad said that Davie was a bit sick too but they would sort him out. I think mam must be really sick, because dad says that he didnt think mam would ever come out of hospital. I dont think that he was lying.

Im really frightened that my mams going to die and that its all my fault that shes sick. I should have looked after her more, instead of going out to fuck Mike.

Its all my fault.

I dont want my mam to die. I miss my mam.
Bye bye.

> > > > >

Hello.
Sues not my mam. Shes Lucys mam and her and Lucy are like best friends. I miss my mam.
Bye bye.

> > > > >

Hello.
<u>No school</u>
Our Davie asked dad if mam being nearly dying meant that we could live with him. Dad gave me an angry look like I had told our Davie but I hadnt. I think our Davie has been reading this again.

Davie stop fucking reading this......//////

Dad told Davie that he didnt know what was going to happen to us and our Davie started crying and then our Davie pissed his pants. Dad took Davie into the bathroom to sort him out. Davie said that dad wasnt sure what was going to happen, because of me having a baby and the house being too small for everyone.
Why would dad say that?
Why would he say that I had to have a baby?
Bye bye.

> > > > >

Hello.
<u>School, but no school</u>
Im having a baby.
I dont know if I want a baby.
What would I do with a baby?
Bye bye.

> > > > >

Hello.
<u>No school.</u>

I miss my mam.
Bye bye.

> > > > >

Hello.
<u>No school.</u>
Lucy and Kyle came back. I have
to share a room with Lucy and our
Davie has to share a room with Kyle.
Lucy told me that I could use her
stuff, but that I wasnt to try on
any of her clothes because I would
stretch them. She asked me what it
felt like having a baby in my tummy.
I said that I didnt know. It didnt
feel like anything. I think the doctor
made a mistake.
Dad played his guitar after tea. He
told Davie that he would teach him
how to play. Our Davie was right
happy. I didnt know the words but
I knew the tune.
Bye bye.

> > > > >

204

Hello.
Dads asked me if I want to keep
the baby or if I want to get rid of
it. I dont know which to pick.
I wish my mam would help me pick.
Bye bye.

> > > > >

Hello.
Dads going to a funeral today. Sue
isnt going with him because she says
that it wouldnt be right.
Dad keeps looking at me really funny
and coming into the room to talk to
me. He says Ive had too much to
deal with as a bairn and he wants
to protect me from now on.
He said that hell make everything ok.
Bye bye.

> > > > >

Hello.
Dads being really strange. He said
that everything would be fine and

that abortions were practically
routine these days and then he put
his arms around me and gave me the
tightest hug ever.
I dont know what to do. I dont
really understand and I wish that
I could talk to mam about it. Dad
said that his mam wanted to come
and meet me and that she would
talk to me about having an abortion.
Dad said that his mam was really
looking forward to meeting me.
Bye bye.


> > > > >


Hello.
I heard dad talking to his mam on
the phone last night. I think his mam
must be foreign because I couldnt
understand what he was saying. I
asked Sue what he was saying and
she shrugged her shoulders and smiled.
Maybe thats why I havent met my
dads mam before because she lives in
a different country.

Bye bye.

> > > > >

Hello.
I asked dad where his mam lived.
Dad told me that he wasnt from
Newcastle. I cant believe that I
didnt know that and Dad said that
he was born in a house in a village.
The village is called Mortney and its
near to Liverpool.
Dad said that I was baptised in
the church in the village he was born
in and that his mam still lived there.
I dont understand why I dont know
any of this. Dad said that his mam is
coming to see me tomorrow and that
I am not to say fuck or piss in front
of her.
Bye bye.

> > > > >

Hello.
My dads mam is a lot scary. Shes

got one of those double names. She
has Edwards like me but she also has
Knight and I dont know where the
Knight comes from. Shes posh and she
coughs to clear her throat a lot. She
sounds a bit like a man. I think she
had been to my dads house loads of
times because she came right in and
went to the toilet before she even
said hello to me. Our Davie was at
grandma in Bykers house because dad
said his mam just wanted to meet
me first.

She shook my hand when she met me
and asked me to turn around. She
said something to dad in foreign and
I didnt understand. Dad smiled at
me so I smiled back. Dads mam said
that dads sister said to say hello to
me. I didnt even know dad had a
sister, but dads mam said Id meet
her when we all lived near each other.
She said thats what families should
be like all living close together. This
is all really confusing. I dont know
where dads sister lives but I think

itd be nice to have a bigger family
and stuff.
I dont know if I even like dads
mam. I think shes a bit strict and
all her words sounds the same. Shes
a bit blah blah. She stayed for a bit
and then gave me 10 pounds and said
shed come again in two days and we
could go out together.
I am going to share my 10 pounds
with our Davie.
Bye bye.


> > > > >


Hello.
what do I call dads mam when I go
out with her?
I dont think mam will like me going
out with dads mam. I miss my mam
so much. Dad wont talk about her
with me. He says Ive got enough to
worry about. I asked him if she was
getting better and he didnt answer.
I think my mams dead and no one
is telling me and Davie. I dont know

what to do.
I havent given Davie his 5 pounds
yet.
Bye bye.

> > > > >

Hello.
Davie asked where his 5 pounds was.
He is so reading this.

# Fuck off Davie..... /////

Bye bye.

> > > > >

> > > > >

> > > > >

> > > > >

Hello.

Dads mam came to get me yesterday
and she drove me into Newcastle.
Shes got a well smart car with
leather seats and electric windows.
We went shopping in Fenwicks and
Primark. She bought me loads of stuff.
Dads mam is really really rich. I
told her that I really wanted to get
some Nike Air trainers and that Simon
Webb has some at school and that I
really needed them. I told her that
they cost loads of money and my
mam doesnt have any money and that
Simon Webb told me that they feel
springy and that they make him run
right fast. Dads mam told me that
things were going to be loads different

and that I would need loads of new
clothes and stuff.
We had sandwiches in Fenwicks
restaurant and then dads mam said
we had to go somewhere else. Dads
mam drove me to a huge house. It
was the biggest house Ive ever been
to but it wasnt really a house.
There were big metal gates and loads
of trees and bushes and then a huge
winding driveway that went right up
to the front door. It was so posh.
I asked dads mam if she lived there
but she said that she didnt.
We went in and there were some
nurses. Dads mam got a frothy coffee
and I had an orange juice. Then a
nurse called my name and dads mam
came into a room with me. There was
loads of posh furniture everywhere
and the doctor told me and dads
mam to sit down on a right posh
chair. I was dead scared that Id
break it.
Dads mam talked to the doctor for
a bit and then he asked to examine

me. He prodded my big fat tummy
and then he said that he was happy
to do the abortion.

He was dead nice to me and he said
that Id have to come back tomorrow
and stay overnight. Dads mam said
that she would stay too and that
she would get someone to come and
do our hair and nails.

I came back to dads and told Lucy
about tomorrow. Lucy is dead jealous
and its so lush. I cant wait to have
an abortion.

Bye bye.

> > > > >

# BLACK
# BOX #01

Flight Recorder
**DO NOT OPEN**

**[55°01'01.54" N 1°27'28.83" W]**

Bedroom. Ana's first floor flat in a Victorian House near
the coast of Tynemouth. The room contains a wardrobe,
a bed and a bedside table. The wardrobe door is open.
The wardrobe is empty. The walls are red. The wallpaper
is ripped and torn in places. The ripped patches vary
in size. The duvet cover is red. There are wet patches
randomly spread across the duvet cover. They vary in size
and wetness. On the bedside table and on the floor next
to it there are fragments of glass that vary in size. The
fragments of glass have rested where they were thrown.
Next to the fragments of glass on the bedside table, there
is an open pair of scissors. On the bedside table there are
two white rectangular boxes. One of them once contained
sleeping tablets. The other once contained painkillers.
Covering the two white rectangular boxes are many

strands of long brown hair.

---

*~what made you change your mind?~*
*~what made you contact me again?~*

[five second silence]

I was eleven weeks gone when you telephoned me.
I was coping.
I was distracting myself. Planning and reading books
about having babies.
I couldn't contact you. Your mother had helped you
to disappear.

*~did she tell you all about my escape?~*
*~did she tell you all about it in your strange backwards*
*mother tongue?~*
*~am i saying that your mother is strange and*
*backwards?~*
*~ma i gniyas taht ruoy rehtom si egnarts dna*
*sdrawkcab?~*

[sound: a throaty laugh]

---

I remember that I'd spent days trying to contact you.
Telephoning at first.

*~i know that i've told you this~*
*~did you know that it was me?~*
*~how could you have known what i was doing?~*

Your number no longer existed, but I kept on
pressing the buttons.
It was automatic. I never had to think about your
number. My fingers instinctively found the right
buttons, but your line was dead.

[sound: sniffing]

Then I started to walk past your flat. I think I
managed a fifteen-minute walk in over twenty
minutes. I would walk thinking and formulating
what I would say to you.
I wanted to talk to you about being pregnant. About
our options.
I wanted you to listen.
I'd walk up and down your street. Your curtains
were always closed. I knew that you weren't there.
Your mother had helped you to disappear.

*~did she find you a safe house?~*
*~can you tell me now?~*
*~please fill in the holes in my memory.~*

I am fading. I am *blink*ing too much.

[five second silence]

And then.
One day. I stopped phoning the number that no longer existed.
And I stopped walking the fifteen-minute walk in twenty minutes.
I accepted.
I think I realised that there was nothing that I could do.
And so I focused on the baby and on having a baby.
And I was coping.

But then you telephoned that you were coming to see me.
And you did.
You used your key. And you came into my flat. And you hugged me.
Not a tight hug.
You told me that it was your **duty** to stand by me.

And that you were going to do the right thing. You said, **I'll give up my drugs**. You said, **it is my fatherly duty**.

[volume: ↑ high]

You used one of your words. **Duty.** It's not one of mine.

---

*Noun:* Duty.
Something that is expected to be accomplished out of honourable or lawful implication.
*Etymology:* Suggested Anglo French. Possibly first found in English in the fourteenth century when a duty was a tax or fee due to a guild or government.

---

You never asked me if I wanted you to do the right thing. You just assumed. But you were right to assume.
And with that returning you gave me such hope.
And I think that I have always lived with that hope.
Whenever you leave I think that you'll come back. I hope that you will come back to me.
I long for you to let yourself in with a key and to hug me.

[sound: a sob]

It's as if I always knew. It's as if I was always
waiting for today.
You came back this time. You came back today. You
came back to kill me, but you left me to die alone.

___

The view from my window is ever changing.
I see the sand. I see the sea. And that image is my
painting mounted in a chipped red window frame.
And tonight.
As the darkness falls.
That painting holds a final memory of you and me.

___

So you hugged me.
I was eleven weeks gone and you hugged me a hug
that didn't quite reach.

*~do you remember that?~*
*~no you don't seem to be able to recall.~*

But you did.

[sound: throat clearing]

My memory is fading. I can feel it falling from me.
I think that we sat together. I think that you were
with a black coffee and me with a glass of water. I
think that my glass had a single chip in the rim.
But I remember the silence.

[silence]

We sat next to each other on my bed, but we never
lay together.
I don't recall why we were in my bedroom.

*~why?~*
*~do you remember why?~*

In my memory I feel just one of each of both of our
knees touching. Nothing else.

---

*~do you remember any of this?~*

You said, **I have something to tell you**.
I remember holding my breath.

[sound: a sharp intake of air]

And then you told me, **I slept with someone else during our time apart.**
You told me a name, but I have forgotten it now.
It was so important at the time.

[sound: a cough]

*~what was her name?~*
*~what was her name?~*
*~what was her name?~*

My memory isn't as it once was. My memory is
fading. The holes are vast. The darkness falls
through the holes. I want to fall through them too.

[sound: distant rumbling of low flying aeroplane]

You told me, **she's older than you**.
You told me, **she was better than you.** I think that
you laughed and injected something cruel into the
sentence.
And you said, **I'll probably still visit her even though
we're back together.**

*~did you tell me her name?~*
*~what was her name?~*

I don't even know if you ever visited her again.

~*did you use a name?*~
~*did you visit her again?*~

I can't remember.

~*please help me to remember before it is too late.*~

I don't know her name. I can't remember.

[silence]

You told me, **she was a dirty slut**. And that, **I like being with a dirty slut**. You told me, **she can make me come by the way that she flicks her tongue around the tip of my cock**.

~*and do you know what happened next?*~
~*no of course you don't.*~
~*how could you?*~

I vowed then. In my head because I didn't want to say the words out loud. But I vowed that I would become a dirty slut for you.
You see I love(*d*) you.

[voiced: I love you]

[volume: low]

But I didn't ever get to be a dirty slut for you.

*~did i?~*
*~you know that i didn't.~*

---

Pip. Your Pip. Our Pip. Never my Pip.
It was all about Pip then.
It isn't any more. She stopped being the focus.
Frau Gothel Sue came along and Pip stopped being
your priority.
You turned your attention to a dirty slut instead.

*~do you have a dirty slut addiction?~*
*~is there even such a thing?~*

[sound: fingertips tapping on surface]

---

Your daughter. Our daughter. Never my daughter.

*~do you remember when we named her?~*

She adores that story. That myth that we have
created around the naming of our first child. She
tells everyone she meets. The pride that she feels.
The confidence that we have given her from an
accidental comment that turned into a name.

*~did pip tell sue the story?~*

Sue.
I can say her name now. Sue your latest dirty slut.
It's only a name. Only words.
Her name is curved. Her name does not fit over
mine.

[ten second silence]

---

*~do you remember that first scan?~*

Seven days after you came back.
The first prenatal scan.
Seven days after you used your key. And you came
into my flat. And you hugged me.

Not a tight hug.

I still think about that first scan.
It stirs something within me. It causes my throat to
ache.
I remember how your fingers wrapped into mine
forming a tight fist.
We had spoken promises then. You were full of
**duty**. Then.
I still remember how the cool gel made me wince as
it was placed onto my still flat stomach.

*~do you remember that wince?~*

It made you giggle. A nervous giggle.
I remember that we held our one breath. And
then the image appeared on the monitor. A black
and white blur of bits and bobs. And we exhaled.
Loudly. And then she showed us the tiny beating
heart of the tiny baby that we had created together.
She said that the heart was shaped like an apple pip.
And that pip of a heart was beat beat beating. And
you said, **you have a pip inside**. And Pip was named.
And no other name seemed to fit quite so perfectly.
Our Pip.

---

*~and do you remember the night of that scan?~*

I don't think that you do.

It was that very night that you told me that it was our **duty** to make sure that the baby inside of me grew and grew.

You used one of your words. **Duty.** It's not one of mine.

---

*Noun:* Duty.

Something that is expected to be accomplished out of honourable or lawful implication.

*Etymology:* Suggested Anglo French. Possibly first found in English in the fourteenth century when a duty was a tax or fee due to a guild or government.

I know that I am repeating myself.

My knowledge of etymology ended with this word.

---

*~do you remember how you defined your duty to me?~*

You told me, **my duty grows from a fear.**

[sound: a laugh]

And that, **I fear that if I enter you then I may hurt it. Him. Her.**

227

Your solution was simple, **we should not make love until after the baby is born.**
Until much after the baby was born.

*~do you remember any of this?~*

The intention was noble. It was out of fear that you would harm your unborn child.
The baby. Our baby. Your baby. Never my baby.

[voiced: unrecognisable words]

[volume: low]

*~do you remember that declaration?~*
*~you don't do you?~*
*~why am i asking?~*

I know that you don't.
You see the decision. **The righteous declaration**. Those words were yours. Not mine.
You offered the words to me and I accepted. And as you spoke those gracious words, they were immediately lost. And somewhere. Trapped within the labyrinth where lost connections wander. There are a couple of lovers. An ALEX+ANA. A you and a me.

For on the night of that first scan.
We stopped being the us that only seven days
before we had tried to stick back together.
We became two separate beings. Pip's mother. Pip's
father.
And you denied the passion that seeped from me to
you.
Poetic.

*~don't you think?~*

I never got to be that dirty slut that I had vowed in
my head to be only seven days before.

[silence]

*~will you fuck me?~*

[silence]

I guess that I am asking for just one last fuck and if
I die during the act, then you can carry on until you
come.

*~does that make me a dirty slut?~*

[sound: a guttural laugh]

---

There is one thing that I have learned. I have
learned it since giving up my studies. I have learned
that you're a man of your word.
When they are your real words.
You didn't enter me again. You did not harm your
unborn child. The intention was noble. It was your
**duty.** You had a strong sense of **duty**.
Then.

[sound: pinging of a filament in a light bulb]

---

*Noun:* Duty.
Something that is expected to be accomplished out
of honourable or lawful implication.
*Etymology:* Suggested Anglo French. Possibly first
found in English in the fourteenth century when a
duty was a tax or fee due to a guild or government.
Those words are rolling from my tongue. No
stuttering. No false starts. No something else.

*~what is the term for when you hesitate, when you
make a noise to hold the floor?~*
*~it's a hm or an er.~*
*~do you know what i mean?~*

[voiced: [b] sound]

[sound: a foot banging on the ground]

[volume: high  ↓ low]

[silence]

---

I think that you were sometimes tender. I seem to
remember the sensation.
I link memory and feeling.
The tenderness came with a kiss on the cheek or
fingertips brushing my shoulder.
Every now and then. And that was fine. It wasn't
that you were being cruel.
Not then.
You didn't stop caring for me. I was carrying
something precious.
So I think that I became something precious too.

[sound: a guttural laugh]

You never stopped caring for that growing Pip
inside of me.
It wasn't as simple as a **duty**-driven choice.
You just stopped putting your penis into me.
That was the only simple thing about it.

---

*~and did you think that i didn't know what you were doing?~*

Those weeks.
Those months.
Those years.
Before you met Sue.
I knew what you were doing. I always knew what you were doing.
You see I found that piece of paper that you had ripped out of a magazine. I found it two days after that first scan. It was a Saturday. You had ripped an image out of one of those seedy magazines.

*~where did you leave that magazine after you had selected your favourite image?~*

I always wondered that.

*~please tell me now.~*

Time must be tick tocking closer to there.
You see I remember that the page was ragged around the edge when I first found it.
But you changed that.

*~didn't you?~*

You perfected the ripped page with your craft knife,
a pencil and a ruler.

[sound: scratching]

You created a faultlessly edged piece of art that you
carried with you. And the image of that blonde girl.
She has stayed with me for all of these years. And
your carrying her around with you, barely hidden
within your wallet. Well that pierced me more than
anything that you and Sue reached together.
I remember the image of that blonde girl.
There are no *blink* holes.

[sound: a hoarse laugh]
[volume: high]

She was everything that I could never be.
She was different to me in too many ways.
And on that sheet of magazine. She was on all fours.

*~do you like to thrust into sue from behind?~*

Her head was twisted to look back over her

shoulder. To look into your eyes. Her lips were
glistening. Her right hand, with her extended index
finger and manicured red nail rested onto her lips.
Her wet lips. I remember.
You see, she lives in my head.
Her legs were spread. Her pelvis tilting her arse
upwards. Opening. Widening her hairless places.
Inviting you into her. And you wished that you
could.

~*didn't you?*~

[sound: laugh to snort]


You betrayed me.
Whenever you were with her.
And what you did to make that ripped image
perfect.
Well that punctured me.
A prick.

~*kind of ironic.*~
~*don't you think?*~

[sound: laugh to snort]

And over time I shrank.
Your relationship with that single sheet of paper was
worse than anything that you could have achieved
with the complete magazine. You'd selected the girl
that turned you on. You'd torn her out. You'd made
her a perfect home.

*~did you think that i never looked?~*
*~did you even care that i did?~*

But where.

*~i need to know where you'd spend your time with her.~*

The two of you together and intimate.

*~did she move on the page?~*
*~could you make her move?~*
*~please tell me now.~*
*~please.~*

Sometimes as I stare out from my black box. I think
that I see her and you on the golden sand. And
she's on all fours, pushing her flawless arse up to
the sky. Her legs open enough for you to stand
above her.

Drip drip dripping a red liquid into her.
I see you both.
But only if I do not *blink*.

[sound: sobbing]

[volume: high ↓ low]

[silence]

---

Red sky at night.

*~is that a good thing?~*
*~or a bad thing?~*

I can't remember.
You'd know that.
You were full of rhythm and rhyme.

[sound: humming of same now vaguely recognisable tune]

You were full.
I can't help but think that my words have a weight
that stinks of context.

*~can context stink?~*
*~tell me about context.~*

*~please.~*

[voiced: blink blink]
[volume: low]

---

*~do you remember what you told me about me and pregnancy?~*

You seem to conveniently forget certain turns of phrase.
My memories are fading but some words are sticky in parts. They cling. They attract dirt and stray hairs.
I used to work with words. I used to live with words. I used to breathe words until they jumped into life.
But that was when I was still me.

[sound: a sigh]
[volume: high]

*~do you remember what you told me about me and pregnancy?~*

I need to stay focused. I need to get to there. From here to there.
You see you told me, **you are an ugly pregnant woman.**

You told me, **you don't suit being pregnant**. You said, **some people bloom, they flourish and they blossom**. But then you said, **you don't** and that, **I'm getting to be rather embarrassed about being out in public with you**. You said, **you're a Red Hag**.

*~you don't remember?~*
*~you did!~*
*~you did say those words!~*

Those words weren't just sticky in parts. They were important words. They were sharp and pointy. They stuck into me. Think human pin cushion but with words instead.

*~but what you're missing is that it's ok.~*
 *~that it was ok.~*
*~you see i agreed with you.~*
*~i wasn't offended.~*
*~i love(d) you.~*

My memories of a pregnant me contain a red me, with twisted features and blotchy skin.
I tried to stop being pregnant. I tried to ignore the symptoms, but I think that Pip wanted me to know that she was growing. And that by turning me into a

Red Hag, she was connecting us. She was somehow
excusing your desire to fuck dirty sluts.
You told me. You told me over and over and over
again. **I am staying with you out of duty. Duty**.
One of your words. It's not one of mine.

---

*Noun:* Duty.
Something that is expected to be accomplished out
of honourable or lawful implication.
*Etymology:* Suggested Anglo French. Possibly found
in perhaps the fourteenth or was it the twelfth
English in century when (*?*)

*~what comes next?~*

I think duty was due to a government or a
something else.

[voiced: my memory is falling]

[volume: low]

[voiced: I'm pregnant]

[volume: low]

But still we remained **duty** bound.

*~was that the point that i was trying to make?~*

---

I remember that the physicals of the pregnancy had started well.

Of course there were seven weeks that you don't know about.

That you never asked about. It was as if the time between your telling me to **fuck off** and your using your key and your coming into my flat and your hugging me.

Well it was as if that time didn't exist.

*~do you still like to be seen as perfect?~*
*~how quickly will you forget my words?~*
*~are they lost already?~*

But even though you returned in body, your mind drifted. I tried to ignore it. I tried to think that everything would be happily ever after. But I knew.

*~of course i always knew!~*

Your eyes told me stories. Your eyes told me sordid tales with crawling naked women and your erect penis.

[sound: a guttural laugh]

I can still visualise your penis. I can trace the subtle differences between it being erect and soft. I can feel the curved ridge between my fingers.

*~i think that i can.~*

But I sometimes wonder if my mind has filled in the *blink* caused holes. I think that I may have made you bigger than you actually are.

*~will you fuck me one last time?~*

[sound: a guttural laugh]

---

*~do you even know?~*
*~why would you know?~*

I hated being pregnant with Pip.
I still remember how much I hated the experience.
I had four months of pregnancy-induced sickness. I experienced actual vomiting after everything that I ate. I went off food. The thought of eating filled me with dread. My food choices were dictated by ease

of vomit.
I remember that during the day. When you were at
university. I chose not to eat.
It was easier.
I'd lie to you about what I'd eaten.
I was clever.

*~yes i used to be clever!~*

You see I destroyed food. In case you checked.

*~do you remember how you'd tell me to grow up?~*

You'd tell me, **stop being so fucking pathetic**. You used
your words. Not mine.
But I couldn't. I know that you don't believe me,
but I really couldn't just click my fingers and feel
normal.
I wish that I could click my fingers now and that I
could go back to normal.

[sound: fingers clicking]

[sound: a sob]

[volume: low]

The pregnancy was consuming me. I couldn't eat. I

couldn't sleep. I hated the sunlight hours. The sun shone into me and made my eyes fold.
I didn't recognise me.
I was ill. I felt like I was dying.

*~i am not exaggerating!~*
*~how do you know how i felt?~*
*~you never asked!~*

[sound: banging of a wardrobe door]

You'd shout at me. I couldn't carry on studying. I couldn't teach my classes. I stepped away from my PhD.
You told me, **you're a hopeless drop out**.

*~i know that those words aren't right.~*
*~they jar don't they?~*

But I can't remember the exact particulars.
I think that you told me, **you're a crap role model for the baby.**
I was ashamed. I still feel ashamed.
But I was consumed. I couldn't function. My PhD stopped being important. My priorities changed.
I long(*ed*) to be normal.

[silence]

That pregnant me was the truest and most purest
form of me. I was exposed and vulnerable. And
I know that you despised me. I know that you
despised that my life had a meaning beyond your
control.

~*didn't you?*~

Now is the time for you to tell me. Before it is too
late.

~*can you be quick?*~

I want to hear the words.

---

It's funny.

[sound: a guttural laugh]

But I still don't recognise me. I don't think that I
could point me out in a crowded room.

[sound: humming of same now vaguely recognisable tune]

And I still long for normal.

*~what is normal?~*

I don't know if I have ever felt normal.
Once upon a time I was normal. I guess that I must
have been.
Once.
It must have been a fleeting occurrence.
Perhaps it was before my mother abandoned me.
Perhaps it was before she withdrew her love.
One *blink* and it was missed. It passed in the middle
of a *blink blink*.

[voiced: blink blink]

[volume: low]

_____

*Blink. Blink.*

[voiced: blink blink]

[volume: low]

_____

*~do you remember how thin i became during those first
four months of pregnancy?~*

I was a Red Hag. All blotches and drained. The
blood vessels around my eyes had erupted from
hours and hours of sickness.

Looking back now it all seems to have happened in a passing of time.

I *blink*ed and I was thin. A thin Red Hag.

I *blink*ed again and I was fat. A fat Red Hag.

But there was a moment. Lost in the middle of the feeling sick. Where I was the thinnest that I had ever been to that date. And although I looked a thin Red Hag, I had the body that you always wanted me to have.

*~do you remember?~*

Of course you don't. You left the room when I undressed.

You stuck to your noble declaration.

I recalled. I remembered. I convinced myself that our lack of lovemaking stemmed from a fear that you might hurt it. Him. Her.

And yes your solution was simple. Perhaps it was too simple. A perfect excuse for you to go out to meet your dirty sluts. A perfect excuse for you to relate to that perfected piece of paper in your wallet.

*~did i say that the intention was noble?~*
*~did i really say that?~*

[silence]

Well I lied.
My bitterness grew inside me.
The baby. Our baby. Your baby. Never my baby.
Even then that baby was joining and dividing.
And I remember telling you that I feared what
would happen when he/she/it was born.

*~do you remember that declaration?~*
*~you don't do you?~*
*~why am i asking?~*

I know that you don't. You never asked me to
explain. The conversation topic didn't develop.
But I was thin.

*~do you at least remember how beautifully thin i was
then?~*
*~of course you don't.~*

You prefer the negatives that you have gathered
inside your head. They fit. You can't allow yourself
to think positive thoughts about me.

*~you should try.~*
*~you should try to have one nice thought.~*
*~go on!~*

*~please try.~*

I will even give you the thought. Try to remember
how thin I was.
My thoughts are wise today.
But they and I are fading.

*~try!~*
*~please try.~*

Before it is too late.

---

*~but did you never wonder?~*
*~of course you never wondered.~*
*~did you even care that i had to replace your cock with
my fingers?~*
*~of course you didn't.~*

I remember rubbing myself till my fingertips became
numb. But without a hard cock my coming never
did quite peak.

[voiced: any cock would have done]

[volume: low]

---

I was a thin Red Hag.
*Blink. Blink.*
I was a fat Red Hag.

---

*~so what do you remember of the pregnancy?~*

I am waiting for you to use the word swelling.
The nausea stopped. I think that I was about
seventeen weeks pregnant.
And then it was as if I was being pumped up. I
became fat. The pregnancy no longer consumed
me. I could eat. I could sleep. I no longer hated the
sunlight hours. The sun shone into me and my eyes
no longer folded.
But still I didn't recognise me.
I remember that I wasn't ill any more. I remember
that I no longer felt like I was dying.

*~or am i remembering something else?~*

Perhaps I am remembering the sweeping wave of
relief, I don't know.

*~do you remember?~*

I don't know.

[silence]

So instead I ate. I ate for two three and four. I was told to eat. By you.

*~you must take some responsibility.~*
*~please take some responsibility!~*
*~do you remember?~*

You kept telling me that your baby needed food. That it was my **duty** to feed the baby. You used one of your words. **Duty.** It's not one of mine.

---

*Noun:* Duty.
Something that is expected to be accomplished out of honourable or lawful implication.
*Etymology:* Suggested Anglo French. Possibly first found in English.

*~can you tell me what comes next?~*

---

I love(*d*) you. I did what you told me to do.

*~i will always do what you tell me to do.~*

I did today. I did then.
You always know best.

*~or do you?~*

I ate for one two three babies. Just in case.

*~just in case what?~*

I love(*d*) you. I would do anything for you. And you
liked to see me eat.

*~do you remember that you would always watch me
when i ate?~*
*~did it turn you on?~*

You monitored my intake. You wrote it down in
backwards language. In your notebook.
I knew that you were doing it for your mother. I
knew that you never mentioned her. But I saw the
notebook. I saw your backwards mother tongue
words. They were ready to be told to your mother.
But I didn't say anything. My eating habits must
have been top of the agenda in your monthly report

to your mother.
I didn't want to rock the boat.

~*rock the boat?*~

There is a linguistic term for that expression. I used
to know it. I used to apply terminology and perform
analysis. Now I don't.

~*now i can't.*~

My memory is fading. I have forgotten what I once
knew.
*Blink. Blink.*

[sound: distant rumbling of low flying aeroplane]

---

I wish that I could see me as I became a fat Red
Hag. The transformation must have been alarming,
as I ate all that you gave me.
You told me what was good for the baby. For your
baby.
And because I love(*d*) you. And because I want(*ed*)
to make you happy.
I ate.

[sound: sobbing]

Then.

One day I found myself with the stretched body of a
fat person.

I was marked with red bands that told everyone
that I was once thin. I became a fat Red Hag. My
skin was splattered with red blotches. Constantly.
Strawberry patches decorated my skin. I wasn't just
swollen, I was fat. My fat wobbled. I remember
my legs rubbing together at the top. They chafed.
They left bright red scratch marks that became sore.
I rubbed Vaseline onto my skin. And the Vaseline
stopped the fat sticking together.

*~did you know that?~*

The red bands became a shimmering silver over
time. I still have them. I think that I still have them.

*~where are they?~*
*~where are they?~*

I am half the person that I was then. I have lost half
of myself.

*~do you remember my bands?~*

I have lost them. They have gone now.

*~were they ever there?~*
*~did you ever see them?~*
*~where have they gone?*
*~where have they gone?~*

[voiced: my memory is falling]

[volume: low]

My memories are fading. My body is dissolving.

---

I remember. I think I remember lying on my bed. I
was cold. I had a red duvet pulled up to my chins.
I think that I remember you had used your key and
had let yourself into my flat. I think that I remember
you entering the bedroom.
I think that you climbed onto my bed and straddled
my legs. I remember you leaning forward and your
stomach resting on the baby bump. That memory is
flavoured with your sweaty scent.

[voiced: hello]

[volume: low]

I remember thinking that you were going to kiss me. And I remember smiling with that thought. I couldn't help it. I thought you were going to be tender. I should have known differently.
I remember you placing your index finger onto my face and that you flicked down as you counted my chins.

*~do you remember?~*

One Two Three Four.
You stayed straddled for a time. I can't recall how long. But I remember your weight pressing onto the bump. Onto your baby. And I remember gasping.

*~was it a loud gasp?~*
*~did i make you jump away in horror?~*

My memory is fading.
*Blink. Blink.*
You stopped stooping. I remember you straightened your back and continued to straddle me. You told me, **you need to continue eating for two three four**. And, **I like watching you eat**. You said, **it turns me on**.

*~do you remember?~*

I remember those words because I remember your smile. You smiled that smile that covered heavy and dark words. I hate(*d*) that smile.

[sound: distant rumbling of low flying aeroplane]

You remained straddling me. I lay flat, with my arms tight to my side. I remember looking up and at you. I remember feeling fear. I didn't know what you were going to do. That was the first time that I felt fear towards you.
It was not the last.

[silence]

It was the first.
You did not touch me in any way. You did not touch yourself in any way. I wanted you to masturbate. I wanted to see your cock in your hand. Or I think that's what I wanted.

*~did you want to fuck me?~*
*~did you even think about fucking me?~*

256

My memories are twisted. I think I have *blink*ed too much.

[voiced: my memory is falling]

[volume: low]

You remained upright and you looked me in my eyes and asked me a question.

*~do you remember the question?~*
*~of course you won't remember!~*

You asked me, **do you know that you have four chins**? You told me, **you have multiple chins**. Then you pulled your notebook from the back pocket of your trousers and stared at the words. Your eyes flicked across the page. Then you stopped reading. You slotted your notebook back into your back pocket and you told me, **you have to carry on eating.** You said, **you hadn't eaten enough for my baby.** You used other words. More precise. With a sharper edge. I can't recall them.

*~why can't i recall them?~*

And then you turned your body to get off the bed.
I remember you climbing from me and knocking
my knees with your heavy legs as you clambered. I
remember my hand clutching my knee.
You did not apologise. You never apologise.
You carried on walking out of my bedroom. I could
see your notebook sticking up from your back
pocket.
And I did as you told me to do.
I love(*d*) you. I would do anything to please you.
I carried on eating.
I want(*ed*) to please you. I want(*ed*) to make you
happy.

*~did i ever make you happy?~*
*~don't answer that!~*
*~do answer that.~*

I think that I need to know.

[silence]

---

*~do you remember when you told me that we needed to
live together?~*

There were never plans for a marriage between us.

[voiced: my memory is falling]

[volume: low]

I remember your telling me, **marriage would be wrong for us**.
You told me, **marriage is for people who love each other**. That, **it is the ultimate connection**. That, **it is the definitive state of being**.
We would never be man and wife, but I so love(*d*) you. I wanted to live with you.

*~do you remember how you explained it to me?~*
*~am i talking to myself?~*

You said, **I have been told that it's my duty to stand by you**. And, **I am going to do the right thing**. You used one of your words. **Duty.** It's still not one of mine.

[three second silence]

I don't have the energy to recall definitions.
My skin is clammy. I feel so nauseous. I need to vomit.
I can't vomit. I must not vomit.

[voiced: I must not vomit.]

[volume: low]

And I seem to remember that I agreed with you.

*~who told you that it was your duty?~*
*~did i ever even ask?~*

I remember. I remember.
**The baby needs a mother and a father.** You used
statistics in support of your claim. **We have a duty to
lay foundations.**
Your arguments were always so cleverly constructed.
There was no counter argument. I never spotted the
holes.

*~who had told you that it was your duty?~*
*~who had forced that word onto you?~*

I don't even know why I never asked. I wonder if
my memory is tricking me. I wonder if these words
are true. My memory is fading.
I think that I am filling in holes.
I don't know fact from fiction any more.
I really don't know. I seem to be telling a story now.

260

*~am i telling a tale?~*
*~am i creating mythology?~*

I remain trapped in my tower.

*~do you have a ladder?~*
*~should i let my hair fall down?~*
*~your children have half of the loaf this time.~*

[silence]

---

*~do you remember four weeks before the baby was born?~*
*~yes the pregnancy is moving along!~*
*~it is what happens!~*
*~the birth was inevitable after the escaping of an abortion.~*

[voiced: abortion]

[volume: high]

[voiced: abortion abortion abortion]

[volume: high]

It was exactly four weeks before your baby was due to be born.

I remember that you were home early from university.

I remember because you caught me lying on the sofa. And you hated me to be lying on the sofa. You said that it curved the baby's spine.

*~i know that's ridiculous!~*
*~but you said it, not me.~*

You were going to shout. Your face was red. I could see the steam shooting out of your slightly pointed ears.

*~in my head i can!~*
*~in my memory you are a cartoon character.~*
*~is this fact or fiction?~*

I remember you inhaling dramatically.

[sound: a sharp intake of air]

And then exhaling and exhaling and exhaling.

[silence]

And then you told me, **I can't put it off any longer**.

*~do you remember what it was that you could put off*
*no longer?~*
*~can you feel the tension building?~*

You told me, **my mother has paid the deposit on a house
for us**.
You told me, **it is all arranged.** I knew that meant that
your mother had arranged it.
I didn't ask.

*~there is still no need to ask.~*
*~is there?~*
*~or is that me asking?~*
*~don't answer that!~*

You told me, **my mother will pay all of the mortgage until
I graduate**.
You told me, **she will pay until I have completed my PhD
and then she will reassess the situation**.
I remember thinking about the word **reassess**. It was
such a power-fuelled word.

[sound: a high-pitched scream]

I hate(*d*) your mother.
I remember that I didn't speak.

263

*~is it possible to remember silence?~*

[silence]

You were rambling. You were getting all of the words out and hardly taking a breath. In my mind I see your face getting redder and puffier and redder and puffier.
I thought you were going to pop.

[voiced: pop]
[volume: loud]

---

I remember that you told me, **the house is a new build. It's been finished for three weeks**. You told me, **it's furnished**.
You didn't tell me who had **furnished** it.
Invisible words are the most dangerous.
It was ready for us.

[sound: a sigh]
[volume: high]

Then.
As you were slowing down and finally breathing,

you told me, **my mother and I expect you to move in three days' time.** You thought, **it's best to be settled before the baby arrives.**

I knew that all of the decisions had been made by your mother. Everything was controlled by your precious mother.

[voiced: money money money]

[volume: high]

Someone once told me that the relationship that a man has with his mother is an indicator. A flashing red light. A Signal.

For something.

But I don't know what that something is.

*~have i said that before?~*

---

The memory continues that when you finished speaking you sat down next to me on the sofa.

*~do you remember how you told me how wonderful your mother was?~*
*~do you remember you referred to her as a feminist?~*
*~do you remember how you said that she was beautiful*

*and generous?~*
*~do you remember my reply?~*

I told you that your mother was a control freak.
I told you that your mother had wanted to murder
your precious baby.

[voiced: abortion]

[volume: low]

*~and do you remember what you did?~*

I do.
I will not forget.
You turned to me and you punched me in the face.
Your knuckles scraped along my chin. Your eyes
flamed. Your nostrils flared.
I had insulted your mother. No one insulted your
mother.

[sound: banging]

Someone once told me that the relationship that a
man has with his mother is an indicator. A flashing
red light. A Signal. For something.
But I don't know what that something is.

*~i'm sure that i have said that before?~*

My words are echoes.

[fifteen second silence]

---

I can still feel the scraping sting stopping.
Each time that I punch myself in the face, I feel that
same scraping sting. The memory and the physical
turn the sting from peak to low.

[sound: a thumping punch]

I remember sitting in silence. I remember my hand
resting on my bump and I can remember the baby
kicking and moving the skin out from my stomach.
I did not speak.
Your words were not invisible. You spoke in angry
tones. Those words I remember. Some words. The
important words that were sharp and pointy then.
They stuck into me.
Think human pin cushion but with words instead.

*~do you remember what you said?~*

You said, **you're ungrateful**.

You said, **you're a fucking ungrateful whore.**

You snatched the phone off the coffee table and you went into my bedroom. I could hear you talking to your mother.

ruoY rehtom si a lortnoc kaerf.

ruoY rehtom dah detnaw ot redrum ruoy suoicerp ybab.

[voiced: ideal woman]

[volume: high]

[sound: a throaty laugh]

You told your mother what I had said.

I struggled to catch the words hidden within your backwards mother tongue. But I am sure that you told your mother that I had said that I didn't want to live in a house that your mother had furnished.

I hadn't said that.

I had thought many things that I didn't dare to voice.

I remember feeling scared. I remember thinking that you were going to leave again and that your mother would arrange for you to disappear again.

I didn't want you to leave.

[voiced: I'm pregnant]

[volume: low]

So I did something that I had never done before.

*~do you remember what i did?~*

I interrupted your phone call. I remember that I
walked into the room. I said your name, *Alex*.

[voiced: alex]

[volume: low]

I remember that you stopped speaking. I remember
your eyes glaring at me.
I told you that I love(*d*) you and that I was sorry.
I told you that I would be ready to move by the
following day.
I remember that you smiled.
You smiled that smile that covered heavy and dark
words. I hate(*d*) that smile.
Then you told me, **leave the room**.

[five second silence]

___

I remember standing next to the coffee table. I remember the rounded edge of the glass top feeling cold against my calf.

*~do i remember these sensations?~*
*~am i really recalling emotions and feelings?~*
*~or am i making this fiction more precise?~*
*~am i trying to build integrity and trust in the narrator?~*

I used to be clever. I am not now.

[three second silence]

When you finished talking to your mother.
I hate(*d*) your mother.

*~i know that i've said that before!~*
*~don't you think that some facts need reinforcing?~*

You came into the living room. I remember you standing with one shoulder resting against the bedroom door frame.

*~was it your left or right shoulder?~*

I wish that details didn't matter. But I feel that I am

270

weakening the memory by not being precise. Maybe
I should just stop.

*~do you want me to stop?~*

My eyes are spilling red.
I need to *blink*.
*Blink. Blink.*

[voiced: blink blink]

[volume: low]

You told me, **my mother forgives you**. And then you
told me, **my mother never wants to see you again**. And
that, **she doesn't want to see your baby either**.
You told me, **my mother hates you**.

*~you can't deny those words!~*
*~how else can you explain that i never saw her again?~*
*~how else can you explain how pip has never met her
grandmother?~*

I am so very glad that Pip has never met her evil
grandmother.

I ma os yrev dalg that piP sah reven tem reh live rehtomdnarg.

~*do you remember what you told me?*~
~*do you remember the clause?*~
~*yes the clause!*~

You told me, **my mother will stop paying the mortgage on the house that we can never afford, if you ever go back to studying your PhD.**

[six second silence]

---

~*do you remember you referred to her as a feminist?*~
~*can you define feminism for me please?*~
~*do feminists hate women?*~

*Blink. Blink.*
I need to sleep.

[fifteen second silence]

---

~*and what about my phd?*~
~*can we talk about it?*~

I guess that this is the time to talk about all that has
been wasted. There won't be another opportunity.
You have seen to that.
Up until that point. Up until your mother's clause.
I had avoided study. The university were relaxed.
They accepted that I had personal issues, but they
expected me to return to my study of the etymology
of contemporary slang. I expected me to return to
my study of the etymology of contemporary slang,
when my brain was less mushed and my body was
more tweaked.
No one gives up on PhD study after two years. No
one is that stupid. No one is that wasteful.
No one.

[sound: banging]

I only had one more year to go.
But I was scared. I was determined not to lose you
again.
So I agreed.

~of course i agreed.~

I moved into the brand new house that had been
selected and furnished by your mother. I saw our

new home for the first time as we drove into the
pseudo Grecian walled estate in Jesmond.
And I loved it.
I didn't mean to, but I loved packing and I loved
knowing that you were coming to collect me in your
new car that matched your new house and I loved
that new house. And I thought that it would mean
that we would live happily ever after.
I thought that you were my handsome prince and
that I would never be trapped in a tower again.

*~i know that i was wrong.~*
*~don't laugh at me!~*
*~i can hear you laughing.~*
*~but how could i not have been excited?~*

I want(*ed*) to live with you.
I want(*ed*) for us to be a family. I thought that I was
beginning my happily ever after.
I agreed to stop striving to be an academic. Your
feminist mother was dictating. She believed that I
had to be a real mother. I was to devote myself to
you and to your child.
And in return.
Your mother would pay the mortgage and we would
live in a swanky new house.

*~a good deal don't you think?~*


I sold my soul.
Because I like(*d*) to please. Because I love(*d*) you.
And you sold your soul.
Because you like(*d*) to please your mother.


*~do you think that you were a disappointment to your mother?~*

[sound: distant rumbling of low flying aeroplane]

---

We lived together. But not as man and wife.
We were waiting for the birth of our child.
I continued to eat. I continued to put on weight.
I am sure that you told me, **it doesn't matter how you look**.


*~you sound rather gentle in that recollection.~*


But those words didn't mean that you loved me
regardless of my shape.
You didn't mean that your love for me was
unconditional. They meant that you actually did not
care what I looked like. My appearance was of no

concern to you.

*~remember to stop me if i am wrong!~*

You always spoke in angry tones. Those words I
remember. Some words. The important words that
were sharp and pointy. They stuck into me. Think
human pin cushion but with words instead.
As the pregnancy reached its end. Your sharp words
made me eat even more.
You see I believed that in eating I was feeding your
baby and that I was being what you needed me
to be. I believed that was my chance to make you
happy.
I love(*d*) you. I want(*ed*) to make you happy.
But in making you happy, I ate until I was fat.

*~there's no other word for it!~*

And you didn't care about me. You didn't care
how fat I became. I was no longer desirable. I lost
myself. I was barely recognisable as feminine.

*~why would you care?~*

You had your lover in your wallet after all. You had

a number of dirty sluts who called you in the middle of the night. You had your mother and her many tongues.

*~did you fuck your mother?~*

And somehow. And somewhere.
In having your baby, the most natural and feminine act that I could do.
Well somewhere along the journey and just before giving birth, my fat stopped me being a woman.

[sound: sobbing]

---

I was wrong not to have an abortion.

[voiced: abortion abortion abortion]
[volume: high]

I should never have had Pip. I should never have had Davie. I should never have sold Muppet the dog.
I am not a mother.

[sound: sobbing]

My life is overflowing with poor decisions.

---

*~do you remember when pip was born?~*
*~did you wish that i had died during childbirth?~*
*~giving my life so that your pip could live.~*

You must remember the birth. You saw the blood.
You saw her coming out of me covered in brown
and red and white.
I remember that I was on all fours.

*~did you think of her then?~*
*~was she in the delivery room with us?~*

I remember my legs were wide apart and my head
was beating into a pillow. The standard hospital
gown was gaping open down my spine. I wanted it
off. I didn't want anything grazing my skin.

[three second silence]

I was naked underneath. You said that my fat
repulsed you.

[voiced: unrecognisable words]

[volume: low]

*~don't you remember those words either?~*

The words didn't matter then. I hated you. Then. I
felt anger. Then. I screamed and I shouted out the
word FUCK as the pain ripped through me. The
room was filled with a darker me. You didn't speak.
You didn't come near to my dirty mouth. You stayed
waiting. You wanted to be the first to see your baby.

[sound: sobbing]

I remember that my whole body was convulsing
with the pain. My whole being shuddered as your
baby travelled out of me.

*~and do you remember why i didn't have any pain*
*relief?~*
*~your memory is selective.~*
*~isn't it?~*

I didn't have pain relief because you didn't want
me to have any pain relief. You told me, **please
don't make a fuss**. You told me, **childbirth is a natural
occurrence**. And that, **there are people in China who have
their babies in fields and carry on working as they do**.
You gave me precise histories and statistical support,
but your words did not penetrate me.
I hated you. Then.

*~was it china or was it a specific indigenous people
whom you used as example?~*
*~where did you gain your knowledge?~*
*~did your mother have pain relief during your birth?~*

I have too many questions to ask. I have had years
of unvoiced words.
I sometimes wonder where your mother found you.
I can't imagine her giving birth.

*~is she your birth mother?~*

You once told me that she had stolen you.

*~do you remember?~*

You were stoned. You were melancholic. I was
startled.

*~is my memory fading?~*
*~have i imagined those words?~*
*~have i demonised your mother?~*

Your mother is evil. Feminists scare me.
I hate(*d*) your mother. Be sure to tell her when I
die.

I can almost see her smiling face as she hears the news of my death.

*~did she tell you to kill me?~*
*~did she order it in backward tongue?~*
*~or could it be that this is the real you?~*

You have finally come of age.

[sound: distant rumbling of a low flying aeroplane]

---

*~do you remember the actual birth?~*

I can still mimic. I can still remember how I pushed and pushed your baby out of me. My private parts stretched and ripped. I am sure that I felt the blood vessels on my face crack and then pop. I know that the pain blazed as I forced her out. I know that I needed the pain to stop.
And so I pushed your baby out to you.
I opened up inside. I stretched. I enlarged.
But not enough.
Your baby split me. And I know that you watched from the bottom of the bed. I know that you looked into me. And I know that you remembered. I know

that the image of me ripping helped you. That image helped prop up something within you.

~*please stop me if i am wrong.*~
~*i have considered this for a number of years.*~
~*please tell me if i am right!*~

You watched the rip that your baby made with her huge head.

~*did you like seeing me in such pain?*~
~*do you like that she pained me as she escaped to you?*~

It's a girl.
It's a girl.
It's a girl.
I did not lift and turn my head to see your daughter.

[sound: splashing water]

---

~*do you remember the clock in the delivery room?*~

The clock in the delivery room had stopped working.
It was stuck. Both hands were stuck between the

ten and the eleven.

No one had realised.

As Pip ripped from me. I assumed that the midwife would turn to announce the time of Pip's birth. I think that I waited for the announcement.

In my memory I visualise silence.

*~can you visualise silence?~*
*~how do you visualise silence?~*
*~is it a pause or a freezing of a moment or a time of nothing?~*

I seem to remember that the tick of the clock was not to be heard.

*~am i remembering silence then?~*

You never wore a watch. You liked to use your inner instincts. It was a family trait. No watches and no clocks in your family home.

I remember hearing the midwife gasp.

*~did she gasp?~*

In my memory she released a dramatic gasp that echoed around the room.

The clock had stopped working.
And so your Pippa entered the world without
recognition in time.
Time did not stand still for her birth. It passed by
unnoticed.
Your Pip was born only in a place.

*~i know that that is significant.~*
*~let's just say that the time was eleven minutes past*
*eleven.~*
*~does that work for you?~*

---

I remember that the midwife asked you if you
would like to cut the cord. I heard you say, **yes**. I
had not yet turned over. I remember drooping on
all fours. I remember something close to silence. I
couldn't hear your words. The noise began to muffle
as the pillow folded around my ears.
Pip.
Pip.
Pip.

[voiced: my pip]

[volume: low]

---

You must have cut the tie from her to me. You must have broken that tie and made her all yours.
She was always yours.
I remember lifting my head. I remember you naming your child. You told the midwife, **we're calling her Pippa Edwards but she'll just be Pip**.

*~does this cause any reaction in you?~*
*~are there any stirrings?~*

The midwife told me to relax. To turn over gently. I think that I remember a pain shooting through my thighs. But I guess that could have been another time.

*~do you ever think of that other time?~*
*~can you even recall what i may be thinking of?~*

I know that I turned my body over and the bloody cord whipped over my thighs. The midwife placed your naked baby onto my standard hospital gown. I remember looking down onto a squashed and battered thing. She was blood splattered and not at all glossy like your magazines had promised. I remember feeling glad that the hospital gown was protecting me from her blood splattered body.

*~do you remember what you said to me?~*

You said, **Pip is the most beautiful baby in the world**.

*~you must remember that?~*

And you said, **I can't believe how perfect she is**. And that, **we have created such a tiny and perfect child**. And that, **we have created something so perfect**. You repeated and stressed the word **perfect** again and again. You were lost for synonym. You were lost for negative words.

[five second silence]

[voiced: pip]

[volume: low]

I didn't think that she was perfect. I have never thought her perfect.
I didn't tell you.

*~why would i tell you?~*

You were emotional. I let you gush the words.
And then you said, **Pip needs a you and a me**. That, **we are going to be a real family**.

*~do you remember those words?~*

Those words have covered me. Those hope-filled
words have drowned within me. You said, **having Pip
makes us a real family.**
I have replayed those words again and again and
again.
I continue to rebound those words off the walls of
this red room.
Those words are trapped within my black box.

---

It's funny how I am shivering here in my black box.
My teeth chatter when I stop to think.
I have no concept of day. I no longer know of time.

[three second silence]

The view from my window is ever changing. I
see the sand. I see the sea. And that image is my
painting mounted in a chipped red window frame. A
sometimes black window frame. A perfect square. A
perfect painting.
The seasons change as I watch.
I cannot tell you the time or the day or the month or
the year.
I cannot tell you the ages of my children. In my

mind they are both eleven.

I do not know my children. I sent them into the woods, but they came back.

They were clever.

I sent them away again.

They exist through that door. They exist on the other side of that door.

They are finding their way in the woods.

My memory is fading and my thoughts are sequencing out of order.

[sound: humming of same now vaguely recognisable tune]

I am backwards forwards backwards. The thoughts are spinning spinning.

*Blink Blink.*

*~what will stop me from feeling dizzy?~*
*~are you going to speak to me?~*
*~are you listening?~*
*~please.~*
*~please!~*

I should stand on my head and count to thirty-seven.

---

One two three four five six seven eight nine ten.
Eleven twelve thirteen fourteen fifteen sixteen
seventeen eighteen nineteen twenty twenty-one
twenty-two twenty-three twenty-four twenty-five
twenty-six twenty-seven twenty-eight twenty-nine
thirty thirty-one thirty-two thirty-three thirty-four
thirty-five thirty-six thirty-seven.
There is nothing wrong with my mind.

*~is there something wrong with my mind?~*
*~do you think that the tablets that you gave to me are*
*beginning to work?~*

The end is nearly here.

*~or has an end already been?~*

---

*~do you remember?~*

In my memory you were wearing a white t-shirt
when Pip was born. When you held her for the first
time in my memory, I see you in white. I think that
you lifted her from my standard hospital gown. But
the midwife was quick to take her from you.
There were things to be done.

*~do you remember?~*

But Pip's tiny blood footprints smudged a splitter
of a splatter over that flawlessly ironed and folded
white t-shirt.

*~but you liked that it did.~*
*~didn't you?~*
*~you liked that you were marked in some small way.~*

You never let me wash that white t-shirt.

[silence]

The midwife must have cleaned and dressed
Pip. Then she must have swaddled your Pip and
awarded you with her. I don't remember. I am filling
in the holes. I think that I had more to push from
within me.
*Blink blink.*
I remember seeing Pip in your arms and I remember
thinking how very petite she was.
She's not now.

[sound: unrecognisable word, perhaps a sob]

I remember focusing on your hands. I couldn't look into your eyes.

I remember making a choice not to look into your eyes.

You see I knew that I would see love. I knew that you were looking at your Pip in a way that you would never look at me.

I love(*d*) you. I want(*ed*) you to love me.

Pip was your tiny bundle. She was squished and squashed. She was battle bruised from her fight into the world. But that didn't alter how you saw her. Her imperfections made her even more perfect to you.

*~do you remember this?~*
*~am i arousing any emotion within you?~*
*~are you even listening?~*

I delivered Pip into your world.
And as I watched your hands clutching your bundle, I saw tiny drips of your tears falling onto the swaddled fortune.
You cried.

*~yes you did!~*
*~please remember.~*

*~i need you to remember before it is too late.~*
*~please alex.~*
*~please remember.~*

I am fading.

[voiced: everything is going to be just ok]

[volume: low]

I remember these images because those drips forced
my eyes away from your Pip and onto your face.
Those tears trickled down your cheek and they
dropped onto your Pip.
They cleaned her.
And with those tears you welcomed her into your
life. And with those tears you claimed her as your
own.
Into our family life. The family that you were
promising her. Then.

[sound: sobbing]

[silence]

*~but you lied!~*
*~didn't you?~*
*~you're a lying bastard really!~*

*~aren't you?~*

[sound: undetectable objects thumping to the floor]

You broke your promises.
You're a lying cheating fucking bastard.

[sound: stomping footsteps on carpeted floor]

You have placed a huge red cross over my
memories. The cross is formed and covering all that
was once filled with hope.
Those memories are nothing. They are false. They
are empty.
Everything is a lie.

*~you liar!~*
*~you fucking cheating liar!~*
*~you know that you're a fucking liar.~*

In my memory you spilled out words in that delivery
room.
In my memory you made promises and you cried
pointless tears.
But your words were shallow. Nothing that you said
had any depth.

When you spoke those words out of **duty**. They
were empty. They were hollow.
They were lost in time.

[voiced: blink blink]

[volume: low]

I wish that I could hate you. Now.

---

My room is a box.
The view from my window is ever changing. I
see the sand. I see the sea. And that image is my
painting mounted in a chipped red window frame. A
sometimes black window frame.
I see your tears falling down down down the
window pane.
The tears that you cried are lost. They are lost in
time.
Time means nothing.
Only place.
I need to sleep.
I need to sleep.
I am so very tired.

[sound: exaggerated yawn]

[volume: high]

I am falling.

*~can you hear me?~*

_____

*~where are all of those tablets that you brought?~*
*~there were so many.~*
*~have you hidden them again?~*
*~did i take them?~*
*~did you see me swallow each one?~*
*~were you here or had you gone?~*

I only know that you were here. I only know that
you came back to me.

*~you were here weren't you?~*
*~you did come back didn't you?~*

You came back to give me gifts. You brought me
my box of painkillers. You brought me my box of
sleeping tablets. You brought me a glass of water.
You brought me scissors and a comb.

*~is that right?~*
*~did it happen?~*

I am losing my mind.
It will all be lost shortly.
My words have no meaning. They are just sounds.

[sound: a sob]

---

*~do you remember when the midwife stitched me inside to out?~*
*~do you remember it was after your pip had ripped me?~*

You won't remember those eleven stitches in and out.

*~why would you remember?~*

I consumed the gas and air. You did not comment.
You were consuming the new love of your life. You were with your bundle.
I remember thinking that I saw your Indian Goddess swaying into the room.

[sound: humming of a now vaguely recognisable tune]

I remember as I breathed in the gas. I remember
that as I sucked and sucked.

[sound: sucking]

I thought that your Indian Goddess was swaying in
beat into the delivery room. In my mind I can see
her dancing with her hips. In my mind I can see her
eyes staring at you with your Pip. In my mind I see
her sadness.
She felt the very same pain that I felt.

[sound: a guttural laugh]

I remember that you rocked your Pip and ordered
my silence when I deemed to cry out in pain. The
pain of the suturing without anaesthesia. The pain
of the mending of the damage that your baby had
caused me.

~*do you remember?*~

I screamed out FUCK and you glared. That one look
from you and I knew of my need to be silent. I had

to stop my noise.

[sound: humming of an unrecognisable tune]

I had to behave as a mother should.
And I did.
I bit my bottom lip until it bled and my teeth left a
dent in my cracked lip.

*~when should i tell you how i felt about pip?~*
*~when should i tell you that i already hated your*
*daughter~*

I have always hated your daughter.

*~why?~*
*~do you even want to know why?~*

I have to tell you.
I hate(*d*) your daughter for making you feel
emotions that I could never stir within you.

[sound: distant rumbling of low flying aeroplane]

I hate(*d*) her.

I was sutured without anaesthesia.

[sound: a guttural ho ho ho laugh]

[volume: high]

*~why is that even funny?~*
*~can you recall the image?~*
*~i know that you can't!~*

I know that you would never have looked my way.
The insides of the channel that brought Pip to you
had ceased to exist.
You had no intention of fucking me again.

[sound: scratching]

*~is raping fucking?~*
*~did you intend to rape me at that time?~*

The midwife finished. I remember her telling me
that I could clean myself. I remember feeling
stiffness, as I swung my legs to dangle from the bed.
I remember standing. I remember feeling lighter.
I remember not quite recognising my feet on the
floor.
I like(*d*) to please. I was happy to prepare myself

for the ward.

*~can you recall any of this?~*
*~am i talking to myself?~*
*~are you listening?~*

[sound: a fist banging on wood]

[sound: stomping footsteps on carpeted floor]

As my feet took my weight. As I began to walk. I
can still feel that trail of blood that trickled down the
inside of my leg. It dribbled down onto the floor. I
could feel the trickling, but I could not stop it. I tried
to clench. I tried to walk faster. I had no control. As
I walked to our maternity bag, I left a pure red trail
of dots behind me.
I remember glancing back to see a dotted bendy tail
that led from there to there.
In my memory I can hear the midwife tutting in
disgust.

[sound: a tut]

[volume: high]

*~did you even hear her?~*
*~did it even happen?~*

In my memory I can still hear her. That tutting noise still rebounds inside my head.

The tut tut tutting ping pongs from there to there to there to there.

My memory is clicking and clanking. I am not sure what is what.

I wish that you would speak to me. I need to hear your voice.

Before it is too late.

I need to hear more sound. The silence is suffocating me. I am falling.

I think I am hearing things. I hear sounds before the visual forms.

I hear a tut tut tutting.

I remember that after the midwife saw my pure red stream and after she tutted in repulsion, I remember the sound of her grabbing blue paper towels from the clanking dispenser on the wall. I remember hearing a rustle and then a clang from a forceful pull.

I am sure that I remember those sounds.

*~can i be sure?~*
*~am i describing the sound correctly?~*
*~can you hear me?~*
*~can you hear me?~*

*~speak to me alex!~*
*~please speak to me alex.~*

[voiced: I love you]

[volume: high]

[sound: unrecognisable, perhaps muffled sob]

[silence]

I think that the midwife ordered me to stay where I was. And of course I would have.
I did.

*~of course i did.~*

I stayed in the very spot and I let the blood trickle from me. I was unable to stop the blood from spilling out of me.

*~do you remember?~*
*~speak to me alex.~*
*~please alex please!~*

I was naked under the hospital gown. I was unable to prevent the puddle of blood decorating my naked feet.
Red.
Red.

Red.

*~you don't remember do you?~*
*~i am real aren't i?~*
*~this is all real isn't it?~*

[five second silence]

But I know that these words are empty. They have
no weight. I know that you will not recall any of
these visuals. I know that your eyes were firmly
locked on your bundle. You and Pip were blowing
bubbles and floating inside them.
I probably wanted to get your attention. I probably
wanted you to realise that I wasn't quite right. I
probably wanted you to see that my insides were
spilling out.

[three second silence]

I have never known how to get your attention.
Even now.
Even when I am dying for you. You are not near.

*~where are you alex?~*

[five second silence]

I remember standing feeling faint and weak and you didn't look at me.

*~i was invisible wasn't i?~*
*~am i invisible now?~*
*~have i already died?~*
*~am i a ghost?~*

I remember standing very still in my red puddle. I remember wanting to lift my feet and splish splash splosh in that dirty blood. I remember wanting to decorate the room in that blood. I remember wanting to dash and splash a picture that would represent all that I could not voice.
I still have no voice. No one hears me.
My children are lost in the woods.

[voiced: my memory is falling]
[volume: low]

I was already on the outside looking in.

_____

*Blink.*

*Blink.*

*Blink* and it is gone. The moment is gone.

I have *blink*ed away too many moments. The normal moments are gone.

I cannot recall normal.

I have memories now that have links in visuals.

My memories are linked with sounds and sights. I have no sense of smell.

Every memory has a purpose. Every memory carries a meaning.

[voiced: sings operatically five gold rings]

[volume: high]


I am *blink*ing too much.

Those memories are fading. The *blink blink* holes are stretching open.

I want to remember what I have already lost.

But I can't.

I can't recall.

*Blink.*

*Blink.*

I am falling. I need to sleep.

[sound: unrecognisable, possibly a groan]

305

An end has been.
I have moved past an end.
Now I am waiting.
I have time to think. I wish that I didn't have to
think.

[sound: a body flopping back onto bed]

In my life I have missed so much. I have never lived
in the now.
I miss the now. I miss all that has gone.
I have *blink*ed away moments. I have hurried them
away.
And those moments can never be recalled.
I have *blink*ed away Pip.

[voiced: my pip]
[volume: low]

I have *blink*ed away you.
I have *blink*ed away Davie.

[sound: sobbing]

Time has passed too quickly and even now when I
know that I am heading somewhere new. And even

now when I know that I can never really return.
I cannot stop myself from *blink*ing.
You see.
It's what I do best.

[sound: laughter]

It's a skill that you have left me with.
I try not to *blink*. I really really try not to *blink*.
But my eyes hurt.
My eyes are red.
Red.
Red.
They are itchy. I need to scratch.
But that scratch is far worse than the *blink*. Each
scratch scrapes away the memory.
My memories are gone forever.
All that is left is a red scar.
A relic from my past.
I am waiting.
*Blink Blink.*
I am falling Alex.
I have lost my life.

[three second silence]

*~is this the time to say sorry?~*

I need to say that I am sorry.

*~where are my pip and my davie?~*
*~are they lost forever in the woods?~*
*~find them alex.~*
*~please find them.~*

---

*~rapunzel, rapunzel, let down your hair.~*

[three second silence]

*~now all their cares were at an end, and they lived happily together.~*

[sound: a guttural laugh]

---

*~rapunzel, rapunzel, let down your hair to me.~*

This isn't how the story goes.

*~shouldn't frau gothel be coming back in to it at some point?~*

I'm telling this all wrong.
I've cast Sue as Frau Gothel, but I don't think the
Prince ends up with her.

*~doesn't he come back and recognise rapunzel's voice?~*
*~don't they live happily ever after?~*

I don't recall the prince fucking Frau Gothel in the
story.
Perhaps I read an older version.
Perhaps the poor woodcutter fucked the dead witch.

*~or did that happen after the horrible mother dies?~*
*~or did he fuck his mother?~*
*~then did they all search chests for pearls and precious*
*stones?~*
*~and then did they all become really rich and happy?~*
*~will money make you happy alex?~*
*~will all the money in the world make your life*
*complete?~*
*~why do i feel that your mother is rewriting the*
*ending?~*

---

*~do you remember the first time that you left pip?~*

I remember you giving her to me to hold. I remember you telling me, **be careful with her**. I remember that you weren't gone long. You had to use the payphone. You had to call your mother. You never told me what she said.

~*do you want to tell me what she said?*~
I remember that when you returned to me your eyes were red. I remember thinking that you had been crying. I didn't ask what you mother had said.

~*can you still remember?*~
~*do you want to tell me now?*~

I used to think that that was when your mother had reinforced her stance. I used to think that your mother had told you that she did not want to see your Pip.

~*how did the rejection feel?*~
~*what did she say to you?*
~*please tell me before it is too late.*~

I promise to listen. I will try to understand. I will try not to say that your mother is an evil witch.

[sound: a guttural laugh]

---

*~do you remember when it was time for pip and me to be pushed in a wheelchair to the ward?~*

It was time for you to go back to the new house that your mother had bought.
It was late. I remember that the midwife said that it was late.
We didn't know the time.
The tick tock ticking of time had no relevance.

*~do you remember that you didn't want to go?~*

You didn't want to leave your Pip. And I didn't want you to go. I didn't want to be left with your Pip.
Time.
Time.
Time.

*~do you remember?~*

I remember feeling sick. I remember feeling sweaty and flushed. I didn't want to be alone with your Pip. Even then. Even now. I didn't want to be alone with

your Pip. With your baby.
I didn't know what to do with a tiny little thing like her.

*~and you knew that didn't you?~*
*~how did you know?~*
*~were my inadequacies obvious even at that early stage?~*

I knew that you didn't want to leave me alone with your Pip. She was always your Pip. You had given her your surname too. Not mine. You had told the midwife her full name. It had been written onto her baby identity bands. It was almost like Pip was not at all mine. Like nothing of her was mine. She was all yours.
She is still all yours. I don't know my own daughter. I don't like my own daughter.

[five second silence]

But they told you to go. And you like(*d*) to obey rules.

*~do you remember their reasoning?~*

312

They said it wasn't fair on the other new mums.
And so you did as you were told. You like(d) to
please.
And I sat in the wheelchair with our maternity bag
slumped on the floor by the wheel.
You left me balancing your little bundle over my
arm and onto my knee.
And I remember you going. You kissed my cheek. A
soft brushing of your lips.
You kissed Pip's cheek. I think that I remember that
your eyes said words. I think that I remember that
I read them. And then you walked to the doorway
and looked back at me. I remember you looking
into my eyes.

*~and do you know what those eyes told me?~*

They told me that you didn't trust me with your Pip
and you saw that I didn't trust me with her.
But you left because you like(d) to please.

---

I remember that it was as I was being pushed to the
ward that I looked down at your baby daughter.
I can still see her now.
If I don't *blink blink*.

If I don't *blink blink*, I can see her in my arms
swaddled tightly in a white blanket. I remember that
she was all squashed and red and not at all like I
expected her to look.
She was featureless.
She wasn't at all like the plastic dolls that I had
instantly loved in the parenting classes. I had taken
one of those plastic dolls home. I had cradled and
whispered to it.
But Pip wasn't at all like a plastic doll and she
wasn't at all like the beauties within your parenting
magazines. Those magazines promised babies with
heads of thick hair, babies with large blue eyes
and with unblemished skin. And your newborn Pip
didn't look right. She wasn't what I expected.
She didn't fit.

*~and do you know what?~*

No of course you don't know.

*~how could you know?~*

I have never said these words before. There are
words that have been locked in a memory and
never been voiced before. There are words that

need to be poured into the open. There are words
that I can and will speak out loud, before they are
lost within my death.

[five second silence]

I have had thoughts and words that no mother
should ever have.

*~how can a mother utter these words?~*
*~how could you have let me be a mother?~*

You see when I sat in the wheelchair holding your
Pip. That first night in hospital. I didn't think that Pip
was the most beautiful baby in the world. I didn't
even think that she was beautiful.
I thought that she was ugly.

I thought that Pip was the ugliest baby that I had
ever seen. And I hate(*d*) that she wasn't perfect. I
hated that her face was featureless. I hated that she
was all squashed and bruised. I thought that she
was unsightly. I thought that her head was huge. I
thought that she should remain swaddled forever
and that that swaddling should reach up and cover
as much of her face as possible.

*~are you listening to me?~*
*~listen to me alex!~*
*~i need for you to hear these words.~*

I remember that as I was being pushed away
from the delivery room. I was thinking. And those
thoughts were loud but clear. I was thinking
thoughts that no parent would ever speak aloud.
But I will. I will now.

*~you are listening aren't you?~*

I'll tell you exactly what I was thinking as I held
your newborn baby.
I was thinking that I would swap her for another
baby.
A more perfect one.
I was thinking that in the middle of the night, I
would find another baby and I would swap her
with Pip. I was thinking about how I would swap
name bands. I was plotting. I wanted a prettier one.
I wanted a baby with a smaller head and jet black
hair.
I felt nothing for Pip.
I am not a mother.

I have never been a mother.
I hate(*d*) her for not being perfect.

[sound: creak of a wardrobe door]

---

The pacing is getting to me a bit. I seem to be
dwelling in a time and a place.
The pacing has slowed. Soon it may just stop.
I don't have time to hurry through my life.
I don't have time.

[sound: distant rumbling of low flying aeroplane]

I can remember that first night as a new mum. I can
remember it all.
I can recall the visual with ease.
If I don't *blink*. I must not *blink*.
I have the visual waiting. In place. In time.
But my eyes are hurting. They are red and I need to
scratch them.
But I won't. I can't scratch them yet. I think that
there is a cat waiting to scratch out my sight. Not yet
though.
My eyes are wide open.
Looking out through the black box. I remain trapped

in the tower. I await your visit with a strand of silk. I await your calling out to me.

*~but i know you will not call my name.~*
*~i know that you will not return until after my death.~*
*~i know that now.~*
*~but still i hope.~*

[voiced: hope]
[volume: low]
[sound: sobbing]

I can see myself on the hospital bed. I am alone. Pip in her plastic crib.

*~you do not share this visual.~*
*~did you go straight home that night?~*
*~or did you visit a dirty slut?~*

My thoughts are wandering away from the visual.
I must remain focused. I can see it all.
I can see a me and I can see a plastic crib
containing the ugliest baby in the world.
I can see. If I don't *blink*.
I know that I did not try to swap Pip. I didn't know

how to remove the hospital bands from her tiny
wrists. And so she stayed next to me.
I never moved.

---

*~if i sing to you will it touch your heart?~*
*~if i give you words and voice will you ask me to be*
*your wife?~*
*~that is how the story goes.~*
*~isn't it?~*

[sound: humming same now vaguely recognisable tune]

*~i know that i'm living in a fairytale.~*
*~i know my weaknesses.~*
*~but this is all that i have to cling to.~*

[sound: sniffing]

---

*~did you know that i couldn't sleep that first night?~*

It wasn't Pip's fault.

*~nothing was ever your pip's fault!~*

I remember that she was swaddled. Her squashed
face buried within a white bundle. I remember that
she slept. And I should have slept too. I was told
to sleep. You'd told me. The midwife had told me.
Your magazines had told me to sleep when the baby
slept.
But I couldn't.
I always found it difficult to sleep in strange places.
It was a trust thing.

*~have i always found it hard to trust?~*
*~did i have lots of issues?~*

I remember that the ward was a communal place.
I remember that there were six occupied beds and
each was separated by a thin curtain. I remember
that there were lamps that could be pulled and bent
over each bed. The ward bedded six new mums
with six babies.
But it wasn't right for me to go to sleep.

*~what kind of a mother would i have been if i had gone
to sleep?~*

You see you had always said that it was my **duty** to
look after Pip. You used one of your words. **Duty**.

It's not one of mine.
The problem was that I had already thought an
evil thought about your Pip. I had already thought
about swapping her with another baby. And as I
sat watching her sleep, I remember that I began to
panic. I remember that I began to panic until I felt
that my chest would rip open.

*~what if your pip died?~*
*~what if she stopped breathing and died?~*

I think that that was when I let my mind wander
into thoughts about her dying. I remember letting
my mind wander into visuals of her funeral and of
thoughts of a tiny white coffin.
It was then that I began to realise that I wanted to
be awake if Pip died. I began to like the thought of
her death and her funeral.

*~what kind of a mother would i be if i slept through her
death?~*
*~am i her mother?~*
*~am i really her mother?~*
*~did i really give birth to pip?~*

I wish I knew if my memory was tricking me.

I wish that I knew if these words and visuals and
memories were true.
I wish that they weren't. I wish that they were.

[three second silence]

I wish that I had been a mother.
But it's too late now.
My realisation and my words are wasted.

[sound: sobbing]

---

Your magazines never told us that the ward was
noisy and that the noise would be constant. It
wasn't that it was the same baby waking and crying.
I remember that the cries of one baby would
trigger those of another. Dimmed lights were being
switched on above beds and through the thin
curtains I could see mothers comforting their babies.
I can see those mothers now.
I can see their gentle rocking as they held their
bundles close.
I knew that those babies were feeding a new-
found purpose in those mothers. I knew that those
mothers were looking at their new babies with

wonder in their eyes. I just knew.
But I wasn't experiencing the wonder of new life.

[sound: a guttural laugh]

I don't believe in the wonder of new life.
I never have.
I hate(*d*) her. I hate(*d*) Pip.

*~what kind of a mother hates her baby?~*

I know that I didn't feel admiration or pride or
wonder when I looked down at Pip.
I felt restless. I felt panic. I felt a need to run away. I
was fidgeting. I was uncomfortable. I was unsettled.
I know that I felt truly alone. I was alone in a
crowded and noisy place.
I know all of this because all those feelings have
stayed with me. I live with those feelings every day.
I am truly alone.
I did not fit in. I have never fitted in.

[sound: sobbing]

I remember sitting on the hospital bed. I remember

seeing a sleeping Pip and I remember fidgeting. I felt that I had an itch. I felt a nagging doubt. I felt a worry that I couldn't quite identify. But I remember it being there.

I had swelling feelings inside my head. I had swirling chaos tripping around inside.

I was tired. I was drained. I know that everything was stirring together.

And I remember as those new babies cried, because that's what babies do. Pip was silent. She did not wake. The lights being switched on and the buzzers requesting assistance and the words being spoken to babies who needed soothing. I remember that nothing disturbed your Pip.

Your Pip slept through the noise. Your Pip slept through the night.

I waited for her to need me. I waited for her to die. I sat with my back against the iron bed rest. I stayed awake.

And as the night left and as the morning came. My fidgeting and my nagging niggle rooted into a new form. Panic grew.

My thoughts are confused.

My thoughts are confused.

My thoughts are confused.

I remember the stirring of panic that I had already
done something wrong.
Then there was the whirring of panic that I was
about to do something wrong.
And that panic made me fear.
Not hysterical fear, rather a fear that had a numbing
point.
The stirring and whirring panic disabled me. I was
paralysed.
I couldn't move for fear.

*~and do you know what i did?~*
*~no of course you do not know.~*
*~you know so little about me.~*

I sat and I listened. I stayed in the exact same spot.
I remember.
I remember.
I remember.
The feelings are fresh. I didn't know what to do with
Pip. I had never held a real baby before her. I had
never soothed a baby. I was waiting to be tested.
I was waiting to see if a maternal instinct would
kick in. And as I passed a sleepless night and as

the midwives changed shifts to begin their morning
wake-up checks, the panic peaked.
I was learning about myself. I was learning that I
had made a mistake.
I realised during that very first night that I wasn't a
proper mother.
I wasn't a natural. I had too many dark thoughts.
I realised then that I had been mistaken to escape
through the backdoor of that private clinic.

[three second silence]

---

I realised that I had made a mistake.

[sound: a loud sigh]

I knew that I should have had an abortion. Like you
had told me to.

~you don't remember saying those words do you?~

I've already reminded you of that memory.

~do i need to say the words again?~
~do i need to bring your mother into this again?~

Your mother taints my memories. I'd prefer to *blink* her out of them.

*Blink. Blink.*

I often wonder what she said when you told her that you had a daughter. I often wonder which words you used.

I evah a rethguad.

*~i don't suppose that you remember.~*

Even now. Even nearly fifteen years on. I still think that I made a mistake. My not having an abortion is the only time that I have ever stood up for myself and I was wrong to do so.

*~yes i am admitting it!~*
*~yes i am saying that you know best!~*

I am telling you now because I want you to know. I need you to know.

That first morning I realised that I should have had an abortion. That first morning and every morning since then I have wished that I had aborted your darling daughter.

*~you never realised did you?~*

*~why would you?~*

I hate(*d*) your Pip. I hate(*d*) a child. I never admitted
those words to you. I wish that I had. Then perhaps
you would have let me give her away.
Perhaps you would have let me give her to a not
pretending real family to look after.
My mother did that. My mother gave me away.

[sound: sobbing]

But we would have found a family that wanted Pip
forever.

*~i know that i am rambling!~*
*~times and feelings are jumbling up.~*
*~help me alex.~*
*~help me.~*

[sound: sobbing]

We could have found a family that wanted to love
Pip and wanted to care for Pip. We would have
found Pip a family that didn't neglect her. We
would have found Pip a family that didn't have
an elder brother who made her sit and watch him

masturbate.

*~i don't care if this is about me!~*
*~i don't care that you don't understand!~*

The words are spilling from me tonight. The
darkness surrounds me.
There must have been one functional family out
there longing for a baby of their own.

*~too late now though isn't it?~*

Everything is too late.
We have managed to fuck up two children.

*~yes i said we!~*
*~you need to take some responsibility for this!~*

I hate(*d*) her. I hate(*d*) my daughter. She is not at all
as she should have been.
She is not perfect.
And had she been perfect, then perhaps you would
have stayed.

[sound: thumping scrape of window frame on wood]

*~the guilt alex.~*

The guilt is suffocating me.
Sometimes I lie on my bed and I think of your Pip
and I feel a wave of emotion sweep over me. I
know all that she has done and how she cares for
Davie.
I know that she needs me. I know that they both
need me.
And as that wave sweeps I long to be a mother.
But then the sweeping wave passes.
And I breathe in my guilt.
I hate(*d*) my daughter.
I should have been sentenced to death. Long before
you did so tonight.

---

You see. I didn't know the first thing about babies.

*~i know that i am stuck on this memory!~*
*~but it is hugely important.~*

You see no one thought to teach me about babies.
And I had no one to turn to for advice and
guidance. Pip was tiny and I was clumsy and the
two things didn't fit right together.

*~so do you know what i did?~*
*~how could you know?~*

That internal conversation was between my God
and me.

*~you want to know don't you?~*

I have wetted your interest.

*~you're interested now aren't you?~*
*~what are you interested in?~*
*~are you even listening?~*

I don't think that I want to tell you. I think that I am
bored by the sound of my voice.
The words are tipped in malevolence.
All of my words seem to be tinged and tanged with
negativity.
I am becoming you.

*~or am i becoming your mother?~*
*~ok.~*
*~ok.~*
*~don't shout at me!~*
*~i know that you don't like me being negative about*

*your mother!~*
*~will you punch me in the face again if i anger you?~*

I know that during those early hours. As the night fell into the morning.
I know that I prayed that Pip wouldn't wake up. I prayed for a punishment.

*~i know that this isn't what i said before!~*
*~i know that my memories are altering.~*

But now I am telling you the truth. I am trying to be honest.

[three second silence]

That night and that morning, I prayed to my God that Pip would die. I prayed that she would slip away as I watched her. And I thought about her funeral and the tiny coffin and all the tears that I would *blink*.
But the tears would not be for the loss of my child. They would be out of relief. A life for an aborted life.

*~don't look at me like that!~*

As I say these words to·you I don't feel ashamed. I just feel sad.
I feel sad that I missed so very much.
I feel sad that I didn't experience the joys of being a new mum.
And I feel sad that I couldn't tell you about it. But you would never have understood me. You never have tried to unpeel the layers of confusion that you created.

[sound: sobbing]


You would have judged me.
Like you are doing now. And like you have always done.
I had no one to turn to and no one to talk to.
I had no one to listen to my words.
I still have no one.

[eleven second silence]

_____

I know what I am like. I know all that I haven't been.
I don't seem to be able to *blink blink* away all that I haven't been.

You see.

I hear them.

They think that I sleep all the time, but often I am curled onto my bed listening to them. They are desperate.

I have made them desperate.

Desperate is not strong enough.

My children live in dread and squalor.

I am evil. I deserve to die. I deserve to be killed.

*~and what do you think of all of this?~*
*~do you deserve to die too?~*
*~are you innocent?~*

I know that if you had not left we would not have fucked up our children.

You are to blame too Alex.

*~accept your blame and embrace it.~*

You still have time to make it better. You still have time to be a father.

*~promise me that when i am gone you will be a father to those fucked up children of ours.~*
*~promise me alex!~*

[sound: water sloshing]

---

When I aborted my first baby.

That abortion that had happened after man number seven and three days before man number eight. I didn't wait to recover from it. I never gave myself time to consider. I know that you know that I had intercourse with man number eight and that his cock dripped my terminated foetus' blood.

Onto my stomach.

I had wanted to be back to normal. And in wanting to be normal and trying so desperately to get on with my life, well I buried all the emotion. I never felt. I never considered.

But during that first night with Pip.

I began to realise that I had aborted a child, not a foetus, not a nothing. I had killed a something and far worse than that, I had never acknowledged my wrong doing.

I had never felt guilt.

I did not deserve to be a mother. I did not deserve to have a child.

And I still believe that my punishment should have been the death of something that could have survived. A life for an aborted life.

I had no right to feel like a mother.
I was a killer whose crime was excused. That is
wrong on so many levels.
I have not been punished for my sins.

*~i need to die alex.~*

I need this to stop.

[five second silence]

---

I can see so clearly. My body is weak. My limbs feel
numb. My skin is clammy. But I can see without
*blink*ing.
Pip has never been how I imagined a child of mine
to be.

*~can i be honest with you now?~*
*~are you listening to me?~*
*~please acknowledge my voice.~*

Pip is not pretty. Pip is not clever. Pip is a fat and
ugly cow.

[voiced: pip is a fat ugly cow]

336

[volume: high]

I wrote that for her to see on her way from school.
I wrote it in huge black letters along the fence.
The fence runs along a footpath, a short cut that
she takes from school. I wrote it in the hope that
it would make her consider all that she was not. I
wrote it in the hope that she would become a better
person. She needs to be perfect for you to return.

[sound: a guttural laugh]

---

I have often thought about my abortion and Pip and
Davie.
I sometimes believe that I love that dead foetus
more than I do my breathing children.

*~i know that i have said that before!~*

You know that my imagination has always been an
active one. I stimulate myself.

[sound: a guttural laugh]

That first night, I thought that if all the six babies on

my ward were dressed in the same way.
And if they were placed in a straight line.
Then I thought that if I closed my eyes and counted
to ten.
And then opened my eyes.
I would not want my own child.

*~what kind of mother does that make me?~*

I guess that it makes me the kind of mother who
aborts the wrong baby and manages to raise
children with whom she has no bond or common
interest.
I do not function as a mother. I do not function as a
human being.

*~why are you laughing at me?~*

[silence]

[sound: a yawn]

[sound: a guttural laugh]

I am pathetic.

---

*~come back to the memory with me.~*
*~please.~*
*~one last time.~*


I remember that I did not leave your Pip alone in
her plastic crib.
I was scared. I was fearful. I was expectant.
I remember feeling panic. I recognised that I was
feeling panic. I remember thinking back to when
you disappeared and those first few days when I
wandered up and down your street. I remember
that the panic that I felt echoed the intensity of that
feeling.
I remember.


*~i really do remember.~*
*~do you believe me?~*


I remember that too many thoughts and ideas were
rebounding inside my head. I remember my head
aching. In my memory I am clutching my head with
both of my hands. I don't know whether or not I
was.
I could not go to the toilet. I needed to go to the
toilet. I was waiting.
All I know for sure was that I had sent terrible

thoughts and evil prayers up to my God. I was
waiting to feel his response. I was waiting for my
punishment.
I was an evil mother. I am an evil mother.
And I remember thinking that if I left your Pip.
That if I went to the toilet. Then Pip would die
from my neglect. And I knew that when Pip died I
would lose you forever. You would never forgive
my neglect.
And at that time, losing you was the worst thing that
I could imagine.


*~don't you think it is funny how gauges shift?~*
*~don't you think it funny that back then i thought*
*losing you was as bad as it could get?~*
*~i didn't know you as well as i thought.~*
*~did i?~*
*~i didn't know just what you were capable of?~*


So instead of going to the toilet, I stayed very still. I
stayed very awake.
*Blink*ing.
I sat on the hospital bed.
*Blink*ing.
I tried to ignore my need to pee.
I stayed awake that night to see if my prayers would

be answered. Curiosity. Fear. Dread. Anxiety. Panic.
Panic.
Panic.
Panic.
I remember that I couldn't move out of panic. I
didn't know what would be for the best.

[three second silence]

The ward lights were flicked on, as your Pip began
to stir.

_____

Time is passing. I am falling.
Yet I still find it funny that I should be recalling with
such clarity.
I still find it funny that those memories are so lucid.

[sound: a guttural laugh]

My eyes are wide open.
I am functioning on supplies of energy that have
been hidden.
I am waiting.
I will not *blink*.
I will not.

*Blink.*

*Blink.*

I am waiting to see.

I am dying.

I am not at all dramatic or hysterical.

I am dying.

I am waiting to die.

I need to die.

My life is not flashing before my eyes. I am not spiralling down a tunnel towards the light. I can feel my body altering. I know that the hours have slipped by. I know that my clammy skin and need to vomit are both connected.

I know that my body is dissolving.

I am waiting.

I am hoping.

My wait and hope all centre on your return.

*~come back and see me one last time.~*

*~please alex.~*

*~please please alex.~*

_____

Pip woke.

*~of course she woke!~*

*~you knew that she would.~*

I wasn't trying to build suspense in my story. I
wasn't trying to grab attention.
The God that views my sins seems to accept them. I
have received no punishment.

*~do you believe in heaven and hell?~*
*~do you think that i will spiral to hell?~*

I know that I am evil, but still I am not punished on
this earth.
I don't understand how religion works. I do not
understand repentance. I do not understand
forgiveness. I do not know of an existence in hell
on earth.

*~do you repent of your sins alex?~*
*~do you seek my forgiveness?~*
*~do you even acknowledge the wrongs that you have
done unto me?~*
*~does any of this matter?~*

I forgive you Alex. Go in peace.
I evigrof uoy xelA. oG ni ecaep.

[sound: a guttural laugh]

---

I remember when Pip woke. Like babies do.
That part is normal. That part of the story you would
expect. You would hope for.
But you don't know the rest.

*~or do you know the rest?~*
*~have i spoken these words before?~*

The midwives may have told you. But I don't think
that they did.
You would have said something.
You would have been angry with me. You'd have
hated that the midwives saw how very weak and
pathetic I was.

*~i am.~*
*~yes i know that i am!~*

And when Pip woke.
I remember that I did not move. I remember that
I could not move. I feared that if I moved, then I
might just pee myself.
And I didn't want that to happen.

I remember that I didn't know my own body any
more. My body had gone missing. And in its place
I had a new and altered shape. A shape that didn't
quite fit with being me. A shape that was turning me
into something else.
My confidence had left me.
You see my confidence had stemmed from my
slimness. My attractiveness. I was attractive. Once. I
am sure that I must have been.
Once.

*~do you remember?~*
*~was i ever attractive to you?~*
*~did you ever desire me?~*

You said, **you were a slut before I met you**. That, **it
became my duty to rescue you**.
Your words, not mine.

---

A slut.

*~how many men do i need to sleep with to become a
slut?~*

I can't help but think that sluts have orgasms.

*~did you ever make me come?~*
*~i can't remember a time that you did!~*

I have come on my fingers thinking about you.

*~does that count?~*
*~does that make me number nineteen?~*

Before you there were seventeen.
You made eighteen.
Since you there have been none but myself.
You remain eighteen. I would prefer you to be
eleven.
I cannot remember seventeen names. I cannot
remember seventeen faces.
I know the number.
You had been keeping count. You had been making
notes and taking details.
And when you decided that enough was really
enough. Then you stepped in with a **duty**-filled kiss
to seal my rescue. Your word, not mine.
You said, **I am rescuing you from a trap**. You said, **you
are destroying yourself**. And that, **I will be your saviour.**
And you did save me from myself. You moved my

place of imprisonment and took away the ladder.
I am a slut after all.

[sound: a cackle of laughter]

---

You see. That morning when Pip awoke.

*~yes i am dwelling.~*
*~yes my memory is stuck!~*

I need to tell you. I need to release these words.
You see that morning I knew that I was wet. And I
knew that that wetness did not come from my pee.
The wetness that came from me was blood wet. I
knew that the dirty blood was pouring out of me. I
knew that my wrong-sized disposable knickers were
wet. My maternity pad had overflowed.
I knew.
I remember that wetness.
But there was nothing that I could do. I couldn't
move. I was incapable.
In my recall I can hear Pip. She was giving a wake-
up call for the other five babies on the ward. A
wake-up call for the other five new mums on the
ward. But her cry wasn't waking me. It wasn't

stirring me into action.
I couldn't move.

*~i know that you don't believe me!~*

I can almost hear it in your voice. But I couldn't
move from the top of the bed.
It was then that the midwife came in.
One of the new mums had heard Pip's distress call.
They had reacted and pressed the buzzing alarm.
They were quick to protect your child.

*~had you asked one of the real mums to look out for
your pip?~*
*~did it involve money?~*
*~had your mother paid?~*

You were always keen to flash your mother's cash.
To show everyone just how much you had.
In your wallet.

*~did you pay one of the proper mums to watch for your
child?~*
*~which one?~*
*~go on, you can tell me.~*
*~tell me now!~*

*~tell me now before it is too late.~*

I need to sleep.

[sound: sigh]

[volume: loud]

---

I've never told you that the midwife came in.
Or that she scooped up Pip.
I never described to you how she placed Pip onto
the hospital bed. Or how that placing was just out
of my reach. And I have never explained how I felt
as she unwrapped the blankets from around your
baby. Her movements were swift and confident.
The midwife told me that Pip had soiled.
I remember considering the word. I remember
searching for the etymology. I knew it. Then.

*~what was it?~*
*~why can't i recall the etymology?~*
*~why won't the words climb onto my tongue?~*

I still consider soiled to be a grown up word. It is a
dirty word.

*~don't laugh at me!~*

I used to be clever. But that was once upon a time.
That was forever ago.

[sound: distant rumbling of low flying aeroplane]

I must have looked blank. A silhouette of a new
mum. No energy. No activity. I didn't respond. I
didn't move.
I remember looking down at Pip's white babygrow.
There were patches of wet pale marks down the
legs and up the back. Her babygrow looked dirty.
She looked neglected.
But she hadn't been. I had been watching her. She
had been asleep. She had been swaddled and safe. I
had watched it all.
The midwife wouldn't have believed me. I didn't try
to explain.
I remember that with sharp expert movements
the midwife replaced Pip into the plastic crib and
removed the dirty garment.
Then she stretched her palm out to me. She
was motioning that she wanted me to give her
something. I was focusing on the length of her
fingernails.

*~i don't know if i was!~*
*~i think that i am filling in description.~*
*~i am stuck in the middle!~*
*~can you help me to reach the end?~*

I remember that I had no idea what the midwife was motioning for. I wasn't trying to be stupid. I used to be an intelligent woman.
I used to be clever. Once.

*~didn't i?~*
*~didn't i used to be clever?~*

I had no idea what the midwife was asking for.
You see she didn't realise that I need(*ed*) words. I needed words.
Words are all that we have. Everything else fades.
Words connect us. They bind us together. They make us rich and fragrant.
I think that my bewildered expression spoke the words that I couldn't.
She spoke, *A clean babygrow. You do have one, don't you?*

[silence]

[sound: a throaty laugh]

I'll never forget the tone that she used. The
accusing tone that powdered the *don't you?* She was
condescending.
She was patronising.
She belittled.
But I still think that I deserved that tone. I didn't
deserve to be a mother. I should never have been a
mother.
I should have had another abortion.

[sound: a high-pitched scream]

[volume: high]

But of course I did have a clean babygrow.

*~are you still listening to me?~*
*~are you still there?~*

You'd packed our maternity bag. You'd have known
exactly where to look.
I remembered starting to move from the hospital
bed. It was as I shuffled to the edge of the bed. It
was as I began to lower my legs. It was then that I
began to realise the mess that I had made.
I remember that the maternity bag was out of reach.
I remember that I had no choice but to put weight

onto my feet and to stand. I remember standing. It
was then that I turned and looked to the bed. It was
then that I saw the snail-trailed blood that I had left
with my shuffle. I saw the bloodstained sheets. The
midwife saw the red sheets. She did not use words.
But I knew that she knew that I was an unfit
mother.
We all knew.

[five second silence]

The view from here to there is red.
I see blood.
Blood is what connects me to you. Blood is what
connects me and you to Pip and Davie.
Pip stole my blood.
Davie was conceived with blood.
I see blood.

[sound: humming of an unrecognisable tune]

---

It wasn't how it was supposed to be.
I wonder if I could alter the memory. I wonder if I
could rework my visuals into something more.

*~something more what?~*
*~what is it like to be a happy new mother?~*
*~what is it like to look onto a newborn baby and feel joy?~*

I remember feeling pure fear as a new mum.
I was truly alone.
I feel that I have always been alone.
Right up until today. Right up until you came back.
Then.
When you came back. I had a moment of not feeling alone. A fleeting moment.
And then you went.

*~are you coming back?~*
*~can you come back to me alex?~*
*~please alex please.~*

---

I may as well ask now.
Well the question is bursting out.

*~can i ask about her in your wallet?~*
*~can i ask how long after pip's birth you waited before taking her out of your wallet?~*
*~did you tell her all about your newly delivered child?~*

*~did you compare me on all fours to her?~*
*~and then what did you do?~*

I need to know.

*~and then what did you do?~*

I want you to tell me. I want to know.
I want there to be no holes. I want to know all
about your wanking habits.

[sound: a guttural laugh]

---

I can feel my eyes wanting to close. I can feel a
pulling motion on the lid.
But I cannot close my eyes to rest. I may not open
them again.
I want my final visual to be you. I am waiting for
you to come back.
If I don't *blink*.
If I don't *blink blink*.
If I keep me eyes wide wide open.
Then the view is red. I am sure that the view has
always been red.
And from this, my black box, I can see the images. I

can see myself in the images.

And the sadness that I feel is overwhelming.

I am waiting to die.

I am waiting to die.

[sound: a sigh]

I am waiting to die.

*Blink.*

*Blink.*

---

And that first pee.

I remember the midwife telling me to go to the toilet and clean myself. The midwife pressed the buzzer for extra help. They would fix my bedding and care for Pip.

I struggled into the toilet with our maternity bag.

The pee. My pee was desperate to flow from me.

I had no choice but to let it.

I never told you about it. I never described the fire. You'd have laughed and called me **pathetic**. Your word, not mine.

But the pain. The pain that I felt during that first pee. My private parts were aflame.

I didn't split open again. I think that I closed up

instead.

I don't even know why I am mentioning that
memory. It has no relevance to this tale.

*~or does it?~*

It is funny how thoughts are triggered and how
visuals bounce into my head.

*~my pee is funny don't you think?~*

[sound: a guttural laugh]

---

*Blink.*
*Blink.*
*Blink* and it is gone.
The moment is gone.

[six second silence]

---

*~do you remember?~*

Three days after Pip was born.
I was allowed to leave the hospital.
I passed the bathing the baby test with you by my

side. You were with me all day in the hospital. You were with me until the visiting bell ordered you to leave.

*~did we talk during that time?~*
*~i cannot recall talking.~*

After three days they were ready to give our child to us.
I remember that a form was signed. I remember that a midwife carried your swaddled Pip to your car.
Your mother's car that she had given to you.

*~what was the colour of the car?~*
*~what colour was that car?~*
*~help me remember alex.~*
*~i need to remember alex!~*

And then I remember the midwife handing a swaddled Pip to you and you placed her into her brand new car seat.
I don't remember you driving. I don't remember pulling into the drive of our new home.
I know that this was to be another happily ever after.
But it wasn't.

Because happily ever after is a state of mind.

~*isn't it?*~

[eleven second silence]

We had arrived at our still new house.
You carried the car seat with your swaddled
sleeping Pip placed within it. And I know that it
was then, that it was with that first step into another
happily ever after, that my guilt crystallised. I
remember a blast of air. I remember that that blast of
air carried a blast of guilt.
It was cold guilt.
It was fresh guilt.
The guilt was alive and breathing.
The guilt was about the abortion that I had had.
The guilt was for a thing that I had done. The guilt
for my daring to dream of a happily ever after. And
with that step into my happily ever after I thought
about the thing that I had had sucked from me.
I thought about that aborted baby that I had killed.
Murdered.
Murdered.
Murdered.
And the weight. And the depth.

And the heaviness of my realisation.
All of those feelings covered me with lead.
And I sank to the ground.
My another happily ever after never began. I never let it begin.

---

*~do you still get your parenting magazines delivered?~*

[sound: a snort]

Even after the birth, your weekly magazines still arrived. You were taking parenting very seriously.
Then.
I didn't have to read them all.

*~where did you get those magazines from?~*
*~were they off your mother?~*
*~i can't believe that i have never asked before.~*

I remember that you'd read all of the magazines and then you'd highlight with a fluorescent yellow marker. You told me, **yellow helps you to remember**.
I've never forgotten that.
*Blink. Blink.*

*~but did you have to go through all the magazines?~*
*~did you never think that i might want to find my own*
*information?~*

You see I remember that all of the highlighting and
all of the sticking of Post-it notes and all of the
folding edges terrified me.
I think back to that time and I feel overwhelmed.
I remember feeling absolute panic in case I forgot
something important. In case I didn't absorb enough
of the information. And I remember worrying that
one day you would decide to test me and I knew
that I would be sure to fail.

[silence]

I failed at being a mother before I even began.

*~no that's not right is it?~*

I think that it should be I failed at being a mother as
I began.
I don't know.

*~alex tell me what is right.~*
*~talk to me alex!~*
*~are you there?~*

[sound: scribbling]

At that time you were determined. You would
never fail at being a father. At that time you were
alert. You never missed a thing. That time was
when you were everything that I couldn't be. A
mother and a father all rolled up into one Post-it-
yielding, highlighter-propelling magazine-absorbing
superhero.
Your super powers were immense.

[sound: a guttural laugh]

---

*~do you remember that you told me that breast was
best?~*

You told me, **giving your breast to Pip will hurry along
the bonding process**.
The breast. My breast was to be given to your Pip
and that would ensure that she received all of my
goodness and in return I was guaranteed a bond.
You must have read it in a magazine. You learned
everything from your magazines.
I think that I did want the best for our child.

*~i know that you don't believe me.~*

I want(*ed*) to please you. I would do anything for
you.
And breast was best.
I remember that it became your daily mantra and
then it became mine.
And so I breastfed. The midwives had helped me to
breastfeed. I had listened. I had learned. But as I fed
Pip in our still new home, she became a leech. An
expanding and demanding leech. And I know that
you knew that she sucked my nipples until blisters
appeared. And I remember that I begged you to let
me stop breastfeeding.
But you told me, **breast is best**.

[voiced: [b] sound]

[volume: low]

Your postnatal favourite words.
And I remember showing you my nipple and how it
had erupted into clear blisters.

*~do you remember what you told me?~*
*~do you remember the words?~*

I remember them.

You told me, **you must be doing it wrong**. You told me,
**you must be forcing Pip to latch on incorrectly**. I am sure
that you used the word **forcing**.

*~i am sure?~*
*~can i be sure of anything?~*

I think that I remember. I think that I am sure.
Because of force being such a brutal word.
It is a word that reeks of pain and neglect.

*~like when you forced yourself into me!~*
*~like when you raped me by force!~*

But ultimately I think that you thought I was looking
for an excuse to stop breastfeeding.
You told me, **breast is best**.

**Breast
is
best.
There
can
be
no
alternative.**

And then one day I remember that I showed you my bleeding nipple.

*~do you remember seeing my naked breast?~*
*~do you remember seeing my blood red nipple?~*
*~did it turn you on?~*

And I know that that was when I told you about the pain. I remember telling you about the absolute pain that I experienced as I fed through the discomfort.

*~and do you remember what you did?~*
*~do you remember how you reacted?~*

I do. You just laughed. Then you told me, **the blood improves the look of your nipples**.
You didn't look me in the eye.
You looked at my red nipple and you laughed.

[sound: glass smashing]

And I know that for the days that followed you continued to laugh at me.
And I remember hearing your words over and over again.

**Breast**
**is**
**best.**
**There**
**can**
**be**
**no**
**alternative.**

[three second silence]

**Breast**
**is**
**best.**
**There**
**can**
**be**
**no**
**alternative.**
**Breast**
**is**
**best.**
**There**
**can**
**be**
**no**
**alternative.**

[sound: sobbing]

But Alex it kept getting worse.
I still remember the pain. I still remember the
bleeding.

*~do you remember?~*
*~you look so blank.~*

---

I can feel you looking into me as if I am telling you
a made-up tale.

*~please speak to me.~*
*~are you there alex?~*
*~are you there?~*

I haven't *blink*ed.
*Blink blink.*
It's a memory. It happened.
My breasts sag into shapeless flaps.

*~look at me alex.~*
*~look at my breasts!~*
*~please.~*

---

*~do you remember when i phoned you at university to tell you about my nipples?~*

Most men would be happy with the topic.

[sound: a guttural laugh]

*~would you like sue to call you at work with talk of her nipples?~*

I think that Frau Gothel Sue would like to converse with you about her nipples and breasts.

*~is she here?~*
*~is she outside the room?~*
*~is she in the woods or is she at the bottom of the tower?~*

I do feel that the art of storytelling is confusing me. I am falling Alex.

*~alex.~*
*~alex?~*
*~please alex please!~*

So I phoned you at university. I think that you'd
been back at work a few days.

*~do you remember my telephoning you?~*
*~how many days did you take off work after pip was
born?~*
*~did you take time off work?~*

My memory is falling.
I think that I remember considering that it would be
easier to tell you over the phone.
I remember thinking about you being in your shared
office with two other PhD students. And I think that
I remember calculating that if the others were there
then you wouldn't shout.
At that time you wouldn't shout in front of others.
That was a time when you liked to keep up the
appearance of a happy home. But we were far from
being a happy home.

*~were we ever a happy home?~*
*~is there even such a thing as a happy home?~*

I can't remember a time when we were happy.
I can't recall a happy memory. I wish that I could.

*~did we ever laugh?~*
*~did we ever smile?~*

I have no memories where my children are smiling.
I do not have smiling children. I do not have smiling
memories of a you and a me.

[sound: a sigh]

*~do you remember the memory that i started this whole
tale with?~*
*~are you there?~*
*~will you listen?~*
*~do you remember?~*

I started by thinking about when we were courting.
I said that I remembered it always being cold. I said
that I was thinking back to when you wrapped your
arm around me as we walked along Tynemouth
beach. I said that I remembered you folding me into
you. I made the image practically cinematic.

*~do you remember?~*

I said that we wore matching scarves. I said that I
had knitted them and they had holes where I had

dropped stitches. And then I said that you had laughed at my fumbling attempt. I said that I had dropped many stitches. And then that you said that you loved them. And that they were perfectly us.

*~do you remember?~*

I said that the scarves wrapped around us. That they bound us together. I said that you could climb up your scarf to mine.

*~do you remember?~*

[three second silence]

But I lied Alex.

*~you know that i lied!~*

I was creating a cinematic hook and a something pretty to pull you into my story.

*~did it work?~*
*~did i make you think and wonder?~*

I wanted a happy memory so much that I made one.

I wanted a happy memory too much.
I long for something happy to cling to.

[sound: sobbing]

---

*~and do you remember what you said to me when i
called you at work about my nipples?*

I remember. I think that I remember.
You told me to, **soldier on**. Your words, not mine.
I remember the etymology. I used to remember the
etymology.
My memory is falling.

[five second silence]

But I did carry on feeding Pip with my breast.

*~breast is best!~*

Because I like(*d*) to please you.
And I remember that your Pip sucked me dry.

---

My breasts sag.

*~look at my naked breasts!~*

[sound: the removal of clothes]

They are shapeless and empty. Their hollowness
makes them flap.
I breastfed away my remaining identifiable
femininity. I breastfed away the weight and shape
of my breasts. I have stretch marks that join into
wrinkles and nipples that point to the floor.

*~look at my naked breasts.~*
*~alex look alex.~*
*~please look!~*

You see I breastfed until you told me that I should
stop. I think that Pip was practically two years old.

*~was she two years old?~*
*~you'll have kept a note of it all somewhere.~*
*~ll'uoy evah tpek a eton fo ti lla erehwemos.~*

And during that time I seem to have detached
myself from my body. I must have floated outside
myself.
The physical me is lost.

I am a voice and words. Nothing else.

[sound: rattle of coins within a china container]

I remember that I continued through what I thought was a cold.
And I remember that that cold became flu. And I remember that that flu became mastitis.

*~you don't recall this do you?~*
*~your silence is a negative reaction.~*
*~can't you at least nod or shake your head?~*
*~you don't remember the red lines that became red hot blotches over my right breast?~*
*~can you remember the hot lumps?~*
*~can you remember my crying out in pain?~*
*~can you even recall the inflammation?~*
*~the heat alex.~*
*~you must remember the heat that poured from me?~*

I am beginning to think that your memories are selective.
I am beginning to wonder if any of this really occurred.

*~are you real alex?~*

*~please will you fuck me or poke me or even punch me*
*in the face?~*

---

*~so what do you remember alex?~*
*~what can you recall?~*
*~what can you recall of those first weeks or even months*
*of having our newborn daughter?~*

I don't mean the photographs. I'm not asking for
a commentary to accompany the stills that you
captured. I'm asking for events.
For recall.
For images.
For facts.

*~what can you recall alex?~*
*~which memories have stayed with you?~*

Recall.
Recall.

*~what do you remember?~*
*~what can you remember?~*

I hear your silence.

[eleven second silence]

---

I wonder why you never read inside of my mind. I
wonder why you never realised how terrified I was.
I think back to my time with your Pip and I feel a
shake. It is an internal shake and a coldness sweeps
over me.

I am cold.

I am shivering.

Nothing can warm me.

I need you Alex. It is nearly time.

Time.

Time.

Time.

*~can you hear a ticking clock?~*

Tick tock.

Tick tock.

Tick tock.

I don't know if I ever panicked before I met you. I
must have. I must have been prone to panic. After
the pain and then with the reality of motherhood, I
remember that I panicked all the time.

*~did you realise that i panicked at everything?~*

My panic was a constant state. My panic was rooted.
It crawled out from my core.
Panic.
Panic.
Panic.
I thought that I was doing it wrong.

*~did you even notice that i wasn't normal?~*
*~what is normal alex?~*
*~tell me what is normal?~*

[five second silence]

Back to defining again.

*~what am i alex?~*
*~did you even notice that i wasn't myself?~*
*~what was myself?~*
*~what had happened to my measure?~*
*~when did abnormal become the norm?~*

I am trapped now.
I was trapped then.
I am trapped within an altering labyrinth.

I don't know my way home. The children were
clever when they left the stones. But not so with the
bread.

[sound: sniffing]

I worried Alex. I worry Alex.
I panicked Alex. I panic Alex.
I remember that I worried that Pip wasn't receiving
enough breast milk.

[sound: sucking]

I remember thinking that somehow my body hadn't
reacted to having her. I really thought that my
body had rejected Pip and in doing so it hadn't
realised that Pip was my child and that I was wholly
responsible for feeding her. I was convinced that my
body was rebelling, that it had realised I could never
be a proper mother.
And that by my body withholding food for Pip, well
I thought that eventually she would starve and die.
I remember hoping and wishing that someone
would be take Pip away from me.
I wanted someone else to be responsible.
I remember wanting someone else to offer Pip a

nipple to suck.
I wanted to sleep.
I still want to sleep.
I am so very tired Alex.

[five second silence]

I was hoping that you would ask me why I never
told you. I was hoping that you'd want the answers.
But gaps and holes never bothered you.
I remember that I couldn't tell you how I was
feeling. I remember the overwhelming feeling of
loneliness. I had no one to share my panic with.
I had no one to talk to.
I have no one now.
When I think back to my breastfeeding time with
Pip, I can visualise me just sitting all day with her
at my breast. I remember sitting in a chair, trying
to keep my back straight and feeling Pip's lips
suckered onto my nipple. I remember hoping that I
would be enough for her. I remember panicking at
all the household chores that were left incomplete.
I remember that Pip would feed for hours.
And I remember being stuck in the same armchair
and in the same position.

*~do you remember that it had to be in an armchair
with my back supported?~*
*~do you remember that you'd read about positioning?~*

I remember that I would spend my days sitting in
silence. Because you said, **my Pip needs silence**.
I like(*d*) to please.
So I would sit and wait for your Pip to finish her
feeding. And you would be at university drinking
coffee with your colleagues.

*~did you realise how i felt?~*

I was lost.
I wasn't coping.
I needed someone to help me to find a routine.
I needed someone to listen to me.

[silence]

My life now is very much like my life then. It is
almost as if the part in between never existed. I
would sit in silence all day then. I would go all day
without voicing a word.
It is the same now.
I used to let the words and feelings rebound inside
of my mind.

[voiced: boom boom boom]

[volume: low]

I remember sitting with Pip for the entire day.

*~i tell you no lies.~*
*~i am not exaggerating.~*

I remember wishing that I had a drink. I remember
walking slowly with a cradled sleeping Pip, into
the kitchen and attempting to make a drink. I was
terrified that she would wake. I was terrified that she
would wake and need feeding again. I couldn't have
coffee or tea as the kettle might disturb her. I longed
for a steaming cup of coffee and daytime TV.
The quiet and the stillness disturbed me.

[eleven second silence]

I remember sitting on the toilet. With Pip at my
breast. I could never pee in front of others. I was so
desperate for you to come home each day.

[sound: sobbing]

*~when did i become so very silent?~*

*~when did i become this me?~*

I remember that I would wait and wait and wait for
a suitable time to put her down.
But your Pip was always a greedy leech. She has
developed into a fat and greedy child.
She was a parasite.
Now she is a cow.
Pip was a parasite who wanted to be on me all day.
I longed to put Pip into her Moses basket.
Now I long for Pip to stay still.
I long for her to not stomp and not cook and not
try to control Davie with her hushed tones. I long
for her silence. With every creak and every minute
sound she startles my mind. She refreshes my
memory. Your Pip reminds me of all that I have
failed to be.
I hate(*d*) her.

---

The Moses basket.

*~is it funny that i should recall that visual today?~*

The start of a life and the end of a life. I seem to be
connecting circles together. I don't think that I have

remembered that visual for such a long time.

*~do you remember pip's moses basket?~*
*~can you recall how it appeared in our home that had*
*that vital clause attached to the front door?~*
*~did i buy the moses basket?~*
*~did it appear as if by magic?~*

I remember it being perfect white cotton. And I am
sure that it was trimmed with a delicate pink ribbon.
It must have appeared after Pip was born then.

*~did we know the gender of pip before she was born?~*
*~did we find out during the twenty-week scan?~*

My memory is falling.
My memory is falling through the holes.
That perfect white cotton Moses basket was a waste
of money.

*~was it a waste of your money or your mother's*
*money?~*
*~or are they the same thing?~*

[sound: rattle of coins within a china container]

My questions are flowing tonight. My voice is strong in the middle and fraying at the edges. I don't think that I ever recall your Pip sleeping in that basket. I know that I could not put her into it. I remember her squawks if I tried to move. I remember how her cries pierced me. I remember how my breasts tingled with each piercing cry. But we'd had to have that perfect white cotton Moses basket. We had to have it. I seem to remember it being on the list.

*~yes your list!~*
*~or was it really your mother's list?~*

[sound: a sigh]

[volume: high]

*~do you remember that you decided that pip should be in our bed with us?~*

I remember you telling me, **I want my Pip in the middle of us**. And that, **I want my Pip to be lying right beside me**. I remember that you wanted to be able to hear her breathing. I remember that you wanted to be sure that your Pip was safe.
Your Pip was everything to you. Then.
I seem to recall something about foreign babies and

other customs and ways of being. I think I recall.
There is something flickering. I think that you'd read
somewhere that Mediterranean countries looked in
disbelief at the way the cold cold British abandoned
their children each night.
And I am sure that something in you understood.
I think that something in you longed.

*~but alex you never thought about me.~*

You never thought that perhaps I would like a
moment without your Pip suckered to my breast.
You never considered that perhaps I would like you
to deal with your Pip during the night.

*~why did you never consider me?~*
*~why did you allow habits to form without adult
consideration?~*

I remember your explaining, **we are a three** and **we
should all sleep in the same place**. **Together**. I remember
you telling me, **that is how it will be**.
And so your Pip and me and you functioned in one
double bed.
Together.
I don't recall when it stopped. Perhaps when Davie

385

was born. But I seem to remember Davie in a Moses basket.

*~davie was never to be in between us.~*
*~was he?~*
*~davie was to be kept as far from you as possible.~*
*~wasn't he?~*

There have always been three in my relationships with you.
You, me and your mother.
You, me and Pip.
You, me and Sue.
I was never enough for you.

*~i wasn't!~*
*~was i alex?~*

Pip made three. Pip made us a three.
Pip.
Pip.
Pip.
Our physical relationship was lost. I was never a dirty slut with you.
And somewhere in that labyrinth where lost things wander there is a me who is getting fucked on a

regular basis.

*~don't you find that funny?~*
*~can't you even smile a little?~*

I was a failure in too many ways.
I am a failure in too many ways.

*~is that why you left me for sue?~*
*~is that why you started fucking sue behind my back?~*
*~tell me alex.~*
*~please.~*
*~please alex please!~*

---

When we were a three I remember waking early each morning.
I remember it still being dark outside. I seem to recall that it was still night.
I couldn't sleep with Pip and you and me in one bed.

*~was it because of the three of us being in one bed?~*
*~or was it rather that i couldn't sleep?*

I couldn't find sleep.

I still feel like that now. Even when I am most tired
I find it difficult to sleep.
I didn't have the energy to sleep then. I don't have
the energy to sleep now.
I remember that I was always tired with Pip.
I was almost beyond tired.
I couldn't sleep.

*~no that's wrong.~*
*~it is wrong isn't it?~*
*~my memory is wrong isn't it?~*

I could sleep in splutters. I could sleep in splatters. I
think that's right.

[silence]

I am falling Alex.
I am falling.
Falling.
Falling.
I don't have the energy.
I can't be bothered.
I need to sleep.

*~help me to sleep alex.~*

*~please help me to sleep.~*

[seventeen second silence]

I'd wake early then. I wake early now.
I wake too early. Sometimes I am not sure of the
length of my sleep.

[three second silence]

I am so drained.
My eyes are flopping closed.
I need to sleep.

*~are you there yet?~*
*~can you hear me?~*

I had too much time to lie and think and worry back
then.
I seemed to glue together with anxiety and panic.
I used to dread Pip waking. I remember that feeling
of absolute dread.
I used to dread the rising sun. I feel this now.
I dread(*ed*) the day beginning.
I hate(*d*) that every day felt the same.
I hate(*d*) that every day demanded the same tasks.

I hate(*d*) the noise.
And I remember that although I was awake in the darkness I would never move from bed.
I lie. I lay.
I developed long-term habits.
I remember listening to you and to Pip.
I remember dreading you both waking. And I remember hating that I dreaded life. I dreaded that another day would begin.
I hate(*d*) myself for my lack of energy.
I hate(*d*) myself for my lack of enthusiasm.
I hate(*d*) myself for my lack of being.
I was not a proper mum. I am not a proper mum.
My life is not as I expected.
I am not at all recognisable to myself.

[sound: sobbing]

---

*Blink*
*blink.*
You see.
Each *blink* cleans your eyes.
I guess that each *blink* freshens them too.
*Blink*
*blink.*

Each *blink* cleans away what has covered my
precious eyes.
Each *blink* removes the now.
*Blink*
*blink*.
A new now replaces the old now.
*Blink*ing is often too easy.
It is too easy to *blink* away your now.
I have learned that you can *blink* too often.
In my life I have *blink*ed too often.

---

I remember being a new mum.

*~let me tell you what it was like being a new mum.~*

I remember spending days not getting dressed and
not getting washed.
I forgot to change my underwear. I forgot to brush
my teeth.
But I didn't forget. Not really.
I just couldn't.

[sound: sobbing]

*~do you think that i am postnatal still?~*

*~can i be postnatal for eight years?~*

[seventeen second silence]

I was then as I am now.

No energy. I was tired. Too tired. My brain wasn't working.

My brain is not working.

I had too much to do. I had forgotten how to prioritise. I didn't know where to begin.

My thoughts were black.

My thoughts are still black.

I had nothing to look forward to.

Every day was the same. Every day is the same.

Each day I was faced with a number of tasks that I had to complete. Each day I achieved nothing.

I remember that when Pip was a baby being washed and dressed was at the top of my daily inventory.

And when the day would start with Pip feeding for two hours, well everything else collapsed into each other.

And I remember how you'd return from university.

And I remember that look on your face. I saw the disgust.

I saw that same disgust today.

*~i disgust you don't i alex?~*

*~tell me alex.~*
*~let me hear the words that long to be voiced.~*

I remember that the house was untidy. The flat is
untidy now.
I remember that washing hadn't been piled into
the washing machine. Washing is not piled into the
washing machine now.
I remember clothes weren't being ironed. I have no
energy to iron now.
I remember that I wasn't vacuuming. I cannot
remember the last time that I vacuumed.
I know that I wasn't even washing myself. I do not
wash myself now.

*~but when did you expect me to do these things?~*

You see Pip was always on me then. And I seemed
to spend my days waiting for her to wake, but trying
to keep her asleep.
Pip was a leech. Pip was a stinking squirming leech.
Then.
I have no excuse for now.
I am an echo of my past.
My voice resonates and rebounds.

[five second silence]

I used to be clever.

---

I remember that there was a day. I remember that
day like a wave.
It rose to a peak.
I remember that Pip was feeding. Again.
I remember looking at her. I think that her features
had started to come out. She was starting to be
beautiful. And I remember seeing how tiny she was.
It was the peak of a wave.
It came. It went.
But the guilt.
The guilt.
The guilt.
The guilt.
I remember the tears and my snot. I could not stop
my sobbing.
I felt so very alone.
I wanted to tell someone how I was feeling.
I knew that I could never be enough for your Pip.
I knew that I wasn't good enough to function as
her mother. I remember feeling overwhelmed.
I remember that I felt trapped in the house. I
remember feeling sure that something was going to

happen.

I know that I started to panic. I remember the rising panic. I couldn't breathe.

Panic.

Panic.

Panic.

I was gasping gasping.

And I know that the more I thought that I could not breathe, then the more panicky I was getting.

I know that I was spiralling. I was falling down and down and down.

In my mind I convinced myself that Pip was going to die and that I was going to die and that you were going to die. I had had a nice thought. I felt guilt at thinking a nice thought about Pip.

I knew that something was wrong with me.

I felt that something was about to happen.

[sound: gasping]

I feel like something is going to happen.

*~why won't somebody help me?~*
*~why won't somebody listen to me?~*

I need help.

I need help.
I need help.

---

I telephoned you.

*~do you remember that i telephoned you at university?~*
*~i know that there were several times that i called you at university!~*
*~i am talking about the time that i was hysterical and called you at university!~*
*~the time after you had told me not to call you at university unless it was an emergency.~*
*~do you remember that time?~*

I remember screaming at you down the phone.
I must have really screamed. I must have scared you. You rushed home.

*~do you remember rushing home?~*

I remember it clearly. The car pulled into the driveway. You came in and did not close the front door. And then I remember that you came over to me and you took Pip. You lifted her out of my arms and you went out.

I didn't know where you had gone.
I didn't know if you were coming back

[sound: sobbing]

I remember sitting by the window waiting for you to return. I remember my eyes searching. I remember how my breasts ached.
I am sure that my breasts were solid. I can still feel how they itched from being stretched full. I remember pressing my arms over my breasts. I was trying to stop the pain. I was trying to make my nipples invert. But my nipples wouldn't invert. I remember the milk that was for Pip gushing from me. The milk seeped through my bra and through my top.

[sound: gasping]

[sound: sobbing]

I remember that it was dark when you returned.

[sound: sobbing]

In my visual you looked me up and down on your return. In my visual you fixed onto my wet patches. You looked at my aching breasts.

I think that that was the only bottle Pip ever had. I didn't give it to her.

*~breast is best!~*
*~where did you take her?~*
*~where did you give her a bottle?~*
*~tell me alex.~*
*~please tell me alex.~*

I have too many holes.

---

*~do you remember when the health visitor came out?~*
*~perhaps you do.~*

Perhaps you will remember something as important to you.
I am sure that you took the morning off university to meet her.

*~did you?~*
*~can you remember if you asked someone else to cover your lectures?~*

Of course the health visitor wasn't coming to see you. She was there to check on me and to check

that your Pip was progressing as she should.
I remember that you had a list of questions for the
health visitor. I remember that she had only just put
down her heavy bag and already you were asking
her developmental questions about your Pip.
I think that you thought that your newborn Pip
was advanced. I think that you wanted someone to
tell you that she was advanced. At that stage you
thought that your Pip was destined for advanced
courses and possibly even a doctorate or three.

*~when did pip's education stop being important?~*
*~when did you realise that she was below average?~*
*~is that when you decided to try again in another
family?~*
*~is that when you started to fuck sue?~*

I remember that the health visitor had questions to
ask me. I remember that she had a questionnaire for
Pip and one for me. I remember that you answered
the questions for me. And I remember that those
answers sounded so precise, but inaccurate.
You told the heath visitor, **Ana is fine**. I remember
that you told her, **Ana is full of life**. I remember that
you said, **I've never seen Ana happier**. And, **I can't
remember the last time that I saw Ana cry**.

I remember listening to your words.
I knew that they were lies. I hoped that you were
telling lies.

*~so tell me now alex.~*
*~did you realise the darkness that i was feeling?~*
*~did you realise and choose to ignore?~*
*~or were you really that unaware of how i functioned?~*

I remember the health visitor leaving. I am sure
that you carried her heavy bag to the car for her. I
remember that she was all smiles.

*~did you suggest a private session in the back of your*
*new car?~*

I am sure that I asked you why you had lied.
I am sure that I can remember voicing the words.

*~did i ask you?~*
*~tell me did i voice those words?~*

I remember asking you why you had said that I was
the happiest that you had ever seen me. And I am
sure that I recall your reply.

*~do you remember what you replied?~*
*~can you recall the words?~*

You said, **they're only words.**
You told me, **you need to get a grip and snap out of your sulk before they take Pip away from us**.

———————————————————————

That sulk went on. I am still having that sulk. And that sulk made you take Pip to every doctor's appointment. And that sulk kept me trapped inside our house.
I had no identity. I have no identity.
I had no friends. I have no friends.
I had no desire to join a mother and toddler group.
I had no energy to pretend to be normal in front of a group of maternal strangers. The invitations to the meetings were left on my answer phone.
I let the red light *blink* at me.
And then I remember deleting them all.
All I had then was a daughter who didn't quite fit right with me. And a you who shared a house and a bed with a me who was lost in an altering labyrinth.

———————————————————————

I miss you Alex.

You see I have *blink*ed.

I have *blink*ed and the years have rushed by.

I *blink*ed and I became a someone whom I don't like.

A someone whom you don't like and a someone whom Pip doesn't like either.

And I miss that man from when we were courting.

I miss the coldness and I miss our walking along Tynemouth beach. I miss me folding into you. I miss the cinematic image.

I miss that life that never was.

I am falling.

I am fading.

And as I do I miss you. I love you Alex.

You are so much more than I ever dreamed that I deserved.

I love you.

[sound: sobbing]

---

When Pip was a baby I found a way to pull myself together.

I was cunning in my deception.

*~you have no idea what i am talking about do you?~*

I could never tell you. Not until now.
I am spilling all as quickly as I can formulate.


[sound: sobbing]


When Pip was small I knew what you already
thought about me.
Your looks said it all. Your look was so full of hatred
and disgust. Then. Now.

*~did you never wonder where i took pip during the
day?~*

You thought that I took her out of the house.

*~didn't you?~*

I'd thought about it all. I'd thought about it when I
could not sleep. The thought of it would fill me with
panic.
I thought about where I would go with Pip. I
thought about my limited options. I remember
considering that by the time that I walked with her
into town, Pip would need feeding. And then I
would panic about what I would do next.
It got to the stage that whenever I thought about

going out with Pip and without you, I could not
breathe. I remember becoming hot and I remember
the sensation of sweat dripping down my back.
But what you don't realise is that I found a way to
deal with it all. I was still a little bit clever then. I
found a way to trick you.
And you never realised.

~did you?~

[sound: a guttural laugh]

You see what I did was I stopped answering the
telephone. I let it go to answer phone. I heard your
messages. And I didn't delete them. I let the red
light *blink* at me.

[eleven second silence]

And then. About thirty minutes before you were
due home from university, I remember dressing Pip
ready to go out. I remember putting her in her warm
all-in-one suit. And I'd put on my long red coat over
my grubby clothes. I remember putting Pip into her
pram and placing it just inside the house. I'd close
the door behind me.

Then.

*~are you ready for the clever part?~*

I used to leave all of the lights in the house off. And
as you pulled into the drive. I'd say that we'd only
just arrived in.
And then you would scoop up your Pip and say,
**she's all cosy and warm**.

[sound: a guttural laugh]

I was playing at being a mum.

---

*~what else do i need to tell you?~*
*~what else can i remember from this time?~*

There are so many holes. The days are one.
I know that when I was pretending not to go out.
I wouldn't answer the door. I guess that that one is
obvious, but I was always terrified that you'd send
someone around to check on me.
I remember that I went one step further than simply
not answering the front door. I didn't want to panic
and I didn't want to hear any noise.

*~so do you know what i used to do?~*
*~why am i asking you?~*
*~how could you know?~*

You see I used to take the batteries out of the doorbell. I used to take out the batteries from the doorbell so that it could not ding. I used to take the batteries out so that I wouldn't have to worry about who had tried to visit. I preferred not to know. Then I wouldn't have to lie to you.
I was still a little bit clever. Then.
And then I remember that I would keep the lounge curtains closed. And I would not open any letters.

*~but you never realised did you?~*
*~did you never wonder why i never spent money?~*
*~did you never wonder why i always forgot to go to the shops for bread and milk and toilet roll and nappies?~*
*~did you just think that i had a really bad memory?~*
*~did you think that i was really stupid?~*
*~did you even care?~*

I guess I spent my days formulating plans and avoiding the present.
And now as I think about it I am overwhelmed with sadness.

I feel so lonely.

That loneliness has shadowed me.

This is the story of a wasted life.


*~there won't be another another happily ever after this*
*time will there?~*


[fifteen second silence]

_____

And finally.

And to my final memory of that time.

And to the one remaining visual.

I remember that there were days when your Pip was good.

As she grew there were moments and hours even, when she was not as demanding.

And I know that those were the hours when I could have done something productive.


*~and do you know what i did during those hours when*
*your pip was less demanding?~*
*~no of course you don't know!~*
*~how could you know?~*


The memory that I have of those moments and

those hours is of a me sitting in Pip's room, with a sleeping Pip cradled in my arms. I can remember sitting in the room that hosted her clothes and her toys. Those toys and clothes that were part of the furnished house that we moved in to. I remember looking into the wardrobe brimming with your Pip's new clothes. I remember reorganising Pip's clothes.

I remember putting outfits and categorising them by colour. And I remember worrying that I didn't have enough clothes for your Pip.
I remember panicking that everything was not perfect.
I remember worrying that I was running out of clothes for her and that soon her clothes would not fit her. I remember worrying that your Pip was growing too quickly and that she would soon outgrow her clothes.

And I became terrified that you would invite someone around. Unexpectedly.
And I became terrified that you would bring someone home to meet your Pip. Unexpectedly.
And I became terrified that your Pip wouldn't have anything to wear and people would know exactly what kind of mother I was. And as I remember

the visual and as I see me panicking, I know that I
couldn't do anything about Pip's clothes.
I remember realising that I couldn't take Pip to the
shops.

[three second silence]

I couldn't go out of the house with her.
So even on the days when your Pip was not as
demanding, the panic within me would build and
build and build.
I need(*ed*) help.

———————————————————————

I have no more memories of a tiny Pip.
I have nothing fresh today.
But I can't move on. I need to move on, but I can't.
I can't move out of the memory. I can't move out of
my memories.
When I turn to the now I will die.
I have been falling falling falling.
I am falling out of our memory and into my death.

*~can you catch me alex?~*

[thirteen second silence]

———————————————————————

I need to sleep.

[sound: slow shallow breaths]

[voiced: I must sleep]

[volume: low]

[thirty-seven minute silence]

*~am i dead yet?~*

---

I still slept naked.
I didn't like to.
But you told me that I should.

*~do you remember telling me that i should?~*

[silence]

I remember you telling me, **boyfriend and girlfriend
should always be naked in bed together.** You said,
**pyjamas and nightdresses are for married couples**.
And we were not a married couple. We were never
going to be a married couple.
I realised that.
I knew.
I think Pip was older when all of this started. I don't

410

remember her being in the bed with us. I think she
must have been about five or maybe four.

*~how old was she alex?~*
*~help me to remember please.~*
*~why was pip not in the bed with us?~*

You made it very clear that you would never marry
me. You told me with actual words that you would
never marry me. I remember that once I blurted
out the question. I remember that I asked, *will you
marry me?* I'm sure that I said, *Pip would like to be
a bridesmaid*. And that, *she would look wonderful
in a princess dress*. I thought that your beautiful Pip
might help influence you.

*~do you remember what you said to me?~*

You told me, **I would marry Pip before I marry you**.
I know that you weren't joking.
You told me, **if you manage to change your nationality
and your skin colour and your shape and then finally your
face. Then I may just consider marrying you**.

*~do you remember the hurtful words?~*

411

[sound: sobbing]

[silence]

You were cruel. Then.

That was the beginning.

---

I did consider how I could become an Indian Goddess. I know that you wanted me to be different. I know that you wanted me to be her.

*~what was her name?~*
*~tell me her name alex!~*
*~tell me her name.~*

[eleven second silence}

*~please alex please.~*

---

In my black box.
I have a wooden wardrobe. It is not attached to the red wall. It stands alone. It stands proud. And inside. Neatly folded. And placed across the wooden base, there is a red sari. A beautiful silken sari that

I bought from an ethnic shop in Newcastle a few
weeks after you left us for Sue.
And every first Sunday of every month.
Between the hours of one and three.
I wear my sari and I talk in your backward mother
tongue.

*~does sue do that for you?~*
*~i don't think sue would be quite so committed to you!~*

---

nI ym der xob.
I evah a nedoow ebordraw. tI si ton dehcatta ot eht
der llaw. tI sdnats enola. tI sdnats duorp.
dnA edisni. yltaeN dedlof. dnA decalp ssorca eht
nedoow esab, ereht si a der iras. A lufituaeb neklis
iras, taht I thguob morf na cinhte pohs ni eltsacweN.
dnA yreve tsrif yadnuS fo yreve htnom.
neewteB eht sruoh fo eno dna eerht.
I reaw ym iras dna I klat ni ruoy drawkcab rehtom
eugnot.

[sound: wardrobe door banging]

[sound: sobbing]

I have changed into my red sari.

[silence]

*~were you even going to comment?~*

I thought it would be the ideal outfit to die in. I
had hoped that my last word would be in your
backward mother tongue, but I am really not sure if
I can.
It all feels a bit staged.
I wear my sari for you Alex.

*~do i stir anything within you?~*
*~do i make you want to fuck me?~*
*~are you there alex?~*

*~are you there?~*

---

We had been together for eight years. We had not
had any intimate contact for five years.
You said, **I prefer it that way**. You said, **you disgust me**.
And, **the thought of fucking you makes me feel sick**.

*~do you remember saying those words?~*

I remember those words. I remember the looks that you gave me and the snarls that increased as the years went by. I didn't realise that you were fucking Sue then. I didn't realise that you wanted out of our life as a three.

[five second silence]

I was stupid. All of my clever had gone by that time.

---

I remember that every night you would strip naked in front of me. You always faced me when you did. I tried not to look at your cock, but I did. I longed for it to be erect and wanting me.

[five second silence]

I remember that every night I stripped naked. You watched. Sometimes you would comment and it was always to point out a flaw or a blemish. You never touched.

I remember that every night our two bodies shared the same duvet. The same cover joined us. We never touched.

415

I remember lying awake and longing to reach
out and run my fingers over your smooth skin. I
yearned to feel your warm flesh next to mine.

I remember trying to make my foot brush against
yours. I remember how you would jump if my flesh
brushed yours. You would be startled by my touch.

*~what was it about me that repulsed you so much alex?~*
*~why did i never feel that you desired me?~*
*~why did you never desire me?~*
*~you promised that we'd have sex after pip was born!~*
*~you did promise didn't you?~*
*~why didn't we alex?~*
*~why?~*
*~was it part or the whole of my body that repulsed you
so?~*

[sound: sobbing]

[silence]

I think that my curves had faded by then. I think
that my breasts had sagged by then. I don't know if
my stretch marks had turned to silver. I only know
that you did not desire me.
I didn't turn you on.

I didn't excite you in any way. I never had the
courage to ask why.
But you excited me.

I could touch myself. I could rub my index finger
gently over my clitoris until I was wet. I remember
my slow finger movements as your back faced me. I
remember touching myself, willing you to turn over
to face me with a hard cock. I remember fantasising
about you turning over. And about your hard cock
pushing into me. And about your wanting me to
come over and over again.

[sound: a sigh]

That was before.

[four second silence]

*~do i need to explain before what?~*
*~are you still ignoring me alex?~*
*~what will break your silence?~*

My stretch marks should bind us. They should

connect us. They should mark our union.
And that union should not have been able to be
removed as easily.
Those stretch marks used to remind me of
ALEX+ANA. I thought that they would tattoo into my
skin and bind us forever. But as my body and mind
dissolve I am left with uncertainty.

[ten second silence]

I don't know what is real any more. I feel that I
have lost my mind.

[fifteen second silence]

I am falling.

---

A betrayal of trust.
Four words.
A
betrayal
of
trust.
Those words tell a story. They send a mind spinning
into a number of narratives.

[sound: sobbing]

*~but where does our betrayal begin?~*
*~do you remember the moment?~*
*~do you remember the day?~*
*~do you remember the hour?~*

I don't.
I can't.
I really don't know.
Because within all of my storytelling the only thing
that I know for sure is that we existed within two
different tales. We don't belong within the same
story. Your voice is not really here. Your words are
not really here.
I love(*d*) you Alex.
But you never loved me.
That story is simple.

[sound: sobbing]

You hate(*d*) me.
And that hatred drove you.
That hatred forced you.

---

I remember the blackness.

[seventeen second silence]

I remember that you woke me from my sleep. I remember that it was not the fantasy that I had dreamed of.

[sound: sobbing]

I remember being woken by the weight of your naked body pressing onto mine.
That memory is flavoured with your sweaty scent.

[voiced: hello]
[volume: high]

I remember feeling startled as I woke. Your weight on top of me was vaguely familiar. I remember a brief flash thinking that you were going to kiss me. And I remember a quick smile with that thought. I mustn't have been able to prevent it. I think that I thought you were going to be tender and that we were going to be happily ever after.

[fifteen second silence]

I think that's what I thought.
But that would be a lot of thoughts within a very
split of a second.
I don't really know what I thought.

I think perhaps I slowed down time.

[seventeen second silence]

I should have known differently.
Your weight took away my breath. And I remember
gasping. It was vaguely recognisable.

[seventeen second silence]

Your sweaty scent was stronger than usual. I
remember feeling confused by smells. I didn't
recognise the smell of your breath. It must have
been alcohol coated without the taste of sleep.

*~how long had you been watching me for alex?~*
*~do you remember this fragment from our life?~*
*~how much consideration did it take before you
decided that force was needed?~*
*~did you sit and plan the best moment for your attack?~*

You should have woken me and asked.

*~why didn't you just wake me and ask?~*

[sound: sobbing]

---

I was still asleep. The gasping because of your
weight and the searching to connect the smells were
first in the memory. My eyes were not opening.
I could not *blink*.
I cannot *blink*.
I have tried to *blink* this moment away. I have tried
to *blink blink*.
But I can't.

[sound: sobbing]
[voiced: our davie]
[volume: high]

---

I cannot *blink*.

[nineteen second silence]

When I don't want to *blink* I can't stop myself.

I *blink blink* away my life.

[five second silence]

When I do want to *blink* my eyes resist. My eyes stay wide open and the action replays in slow motion across my eyes.

[fifteen second silence]

I want to *blink*.

[volume: high]

*~help me to blink alex.~*
*~please help me to make this stop!~*
*~i don't want this now.~*
*~i don't want to end with this.~*

[sound: sobbing]
[fifteen second silence]

---

I am falling into this memory. I want to *blink*.

[seventeen second silence]

I want to *blink*.

[five second silence]

I want to *blink*.

---

We had a history.
We have a history.
We had created a history.

[three second silence]

We were a family. We were three. We were joined
by your Pip.

We were living as a unit. We had a home. We were
functioning in our home.

[five second silence]

*~you know that it was your home!~*

[eleven second silence]

*~please don't say that it wasn't our home!~*

[seven second silence]

*~please don't take that from me.~*

[eleven second silence]

I love(*d*) you Alex.
I really love(*d*) you.
I had (*have*) always love(*d*) you.

I love(*d*) you more than I love(*d*) Pip.

[nine second silence]

I say those words and you look at me with such
disgust.

[eleven second silence]

*~i can feel your eyes burning into me.~*
*~don't you want me to tell you the truth?~*

[nineteen second silence]

I know that you loved your Pip. Back then she was
your princess. She was your everything.
And I hate(*d*) her.
I hate(*d*) that you love(*d*) her.
That she was your everything.

That I was your nothing.

[seventeen second silence]

It was wrong.

[nine second silence]

You made it all wrong. It wasn't how it was
supposed to be.

[sound: sobbing]

We existed. We lived in the same house. We were a
three. We could have lived happily ever after with
your Pip in the middle of us.

[sound: sobbing]

I would have functioned with your outstretched

arms touching your Pip. I had accepted that they were not for me.

[nine second silence]

*~help me to blink alex!~*
*~help me to blink alex.~*

---

A parent's love.
Explain to me a parent's love.
Talk to me about boundaries. Talk to me about unconditional.
The lines are blurred.
Tell me what is right. Tell me what is wrong.
I don't know.
I have no parental love. I have been abandoned.
And when I think of your love for your mother I am even more confused.

[five second silence]

*~did you give her up?~*
*~did you really never see her again?~*
*~did she really reject your pip because she was part of me?~*

Caroline Smailes

[seven second silence]

But she was never part of me Alex.
She was always yours.
Always.

[sound: sobbing]

---

Someone once told me that the relationship that a
man has with his mother is an indicator. A flashing
red light. A Signal. For something.
But I don't know what that something is.

[nineteen second silence]

I am falling.

[seven second silence]

I wish that I could remember more. I wish that I
could *blink* away the memory that I am hovering on.
I am falling into it.

[eleven second silence]

I cannot stop myself.

*~did you have sex with your mother?~*

I know that I've asked that question before.
But you didn't answer me then.

*~will you answer me now?~*

[eleven second silence]

---

I want(*ed*) to make you happy. And as Pip grew I
became an unmarried wife.
I spent my days cooking and cleaning and making
everything seem just perfect.
But that didn't make you smile.

I could not make you happy.

[eleven second silence]

*~i know that i am clinging!~*
*~i know that i am stopping myself from falling into the
memory.~*

*~why can't i blink?~*

[fifteen second silence]

I would have given you sex. I would have
performed. I want(*ed*) to be a dirty slut. I would
have made you come with my mouth.
I would have flicked my tongue around the tip of
your cock.

If you had asked. If you had only asked. If you had
wanted to ask.

*~but you didn't ask did you alex?~*

[seven second silence]

Because the physical never returned in that way. It
stopped within pregnancy. It was under the guise of
protection for your newborn child. And I think that I
somehow expected it to return.
I so want(*ed*) it to return.
I want(*ed*) us to communicate with our bodies.
To be intimate.

[fifteen second silence]

But you didn't want to make love to me.
You didn't want an intimate relationship.
And I know that if I tried to talk to you about us or
about love or about a future or about the physical.
Then you would shout at me.

[thirteen second silence]

I remember you would go red. I remember steam
coming out of your slightly pointed ears. In my
memories you are practically cartoon-like.

I remember your saying, **the thought of entering you
fills me with disgust**. You said, **your smell and your taste
turn my stomach**.

You once said, **you make me want to vomit**.

You once asked me, **would it turn you on if I entered
you and then vomited onto your stomach?**

~*do you remember asking the question?*~

I didn't answer.

[fifteen second silence]

I didn't think that you really wanted to hear my answer.
It would have been, *yes.*

    *~yes.~*

[nineteen second silence]

You entering me and then vomiting onto my stomach would have turned me on.

---

I never told you my fears. I never shared my intimate secrets.
I have so many desires.
I crave intimacy. I crave orgasms.

[seven second silence]

I long for you Alex.

[nine second silence]

Because somehow twisted within all of this wreckage, I want to protect you.

*~what else can i do to make you think just one positive
thought of me?~*
*~just one alex.~*
*~just one!~*

I never shared with anyone just what you did to me.
But now I can't *blink*.
And I need to say those words.
I need to make sense of the memory.
It is confused.
I have unvoiced questions. I am confused.

[five second silence]

---

*~why alex?~*
*~is that an oversimplification?~*

That one word. That, *why*.

A single word sentence. A single word question.
Simple.

*~can you find the words to answer my question?~*

[five second silence]

433

*~why did you open the red paint pot?~*
*~why did you smear the thick red paint all over the*
*memories of you and me?~*

[eleven second silence]

You humiliated me Alex.

[eleven second silence]

*~did you enjoy humiliating me?~*
*~why didn't you just ask?~*

[seven second silence]

I would have said, *yes*.

———————————————————————

I remember that you came so very quickly that time.
You never came quickly. I can count on my right
hand the number of times that I have seen your
sperm.

[sound: a sigh]

434

Tell me the images that were stuck in front of your eyes.

*~what excited you?~*

Because something did. I know that something did.

*~will you watch me as i strip from this sari down to my stretch marks?~*
*~will you let me lie here naked?~*
*~let me pretend to be asleep for you.~*

[five second silence]

*~now will you tell me your story?~*

I will not *blink*. I cannot *blink*.

---

In the centre of a relationship there is a core.
Every relationship has a core. Every relationship has a starting point.
It is a something that can be measured. It is a something that carries a strength or a weakness.

The core of our relationship is red.

435

Every core is red.
It is the centre.
It is the thing from which everything must spiral out.

~*do you agree?*~

The core is that life-generating thing. The core is
vibrantly beating. And this beating does not alter
with the measure of strength or weakness.

[sound: a gasp]

[nineteen second silence]

It is red.

[voiced: I am falling falling falling]

[volume: low]

[voiced: I must sleep]

[volume: low]

[nineteen second silence]

You see you scraped that pulsating core.
With one forceful act.
When you raped me.

You scratched that core until you drew blood.
You scratched the core until you caused an
infection.

[eleven second silence]

And from that day the core became covered in
seeping weeping wounds.

And from those wounds an oozing blood is wasted.

[eleven second silence]

The core will never heal.

---

With you it was always about coercion. With you it
was never about words and feelings. My memories
of you spiral out of reactions to expressions and eye
contact.
I remember few of your words.

[sound: a sharp intake of air]

I remember knowing that something was altering between us.
I remember my instincts screaming inside my head.
The change had been noted.
I remember feeling unease.
And before I went to bed.

On that day.

I remember that you had penetrated me with your eyes. I don't recall any words. I remember that you scared me with your glaring and your staring.

I do remember words.

[voiced: my memory is fading]

[volume: low]

[sound: slow shallow breaths]

[voiced: I must sleep]

[volume: low]

[eleven second silence]

I remember telling you, *I'm going to bed*.
And I remember you saying, **fine**.

[voiced: fine]

[volume: high]

You never said, **fine**.

You always said that you would lock up and follow me upstairs.

It was routine. It was what we always did.

But it changed.

[five second silence]

---

*~and then everything changed didn't it?~*
*~why alex?~*
*~why did you make it all end?~*
*~why did you make sure that there would never be a happily ever after?~*
*~why alex why?~*

[seven second silence]

You threw the red paint over our life. And the story is covered in red.

I cannot *blink*. I cannot *blink*.

I cannot *blink* away the redness.

[eleven second silence]

I cannot *blink* away your memory.

This is not how my fairytale should end.

[sound: sobbing]

---

You used force.
I know that you had been thinking about it before
the act. I know that it was premeditated.
My instincts had been screaming.
You were planning to do something.

*~but what spurred you?~*
*~what was the trigger?~*

There is always a trigger.

*~did you consider the consequences of the act?~*
*~was that the trigger?~*

I have thought about it. I have tried to recall the
days before.

I have tried to think about what made you rape me.

I have had nearly nine years to think. It has taken
me until this moment.

[sound: gasping for breath]

It is now Alex. Now I think that I understand.

[sound: sobbing]

In my head and in my heart I can't help but think
that the thing that drove you was the realisation that
with that one act. With the doing of that forceful act.
You were throwing red. Throwing red paint over us.

And that nothing would ever remove the red.

It soaked into our flesh.
We became black.
And with that one act you guaranteed that the
happily ever after would never happen.

You gave yourself an exit out of the labyrinth.
But with that one act you trapped me in this black
box.

[nineteen second silence]

---

You were communicating with force.

*~your violent fucking was a conversation wasn't it?~*

You were a frustrated child. You were
communicating in the only way that you could.

*~should i blame your mother?~*
*~did she tell you to do it?~*
*~did ehs llet uoy ot od ti?~*

I don't hate you Alex.
I have managed to make sense of it all.

[seven second silence]

*~but why didn't you use words alex?~*
*~why didn't you ask and communicate instead?~*

[seventeen second silence]

Words can be forgotten. Words can be altered.
Words can be *blink*ed away.
But not the memory that you planted with your
force. That memory is buried into my eyes.
I cannot *blink blink*.

[eleven second silence]

---

*~and the consequence of your violent act?~*

You know the consequences. You know that every
act has consequences.

*~are you ignoring the consequences of actions today?~*

Not today Alex.
Not today.
Today we are using words.
With that one act you took away the safety of my
home. With that one act you broke our bond and
you snapped our ties.

[sound: wood or possibly cane snapping]

And I don't understand why. I don't understand why

you felt that you had to use such force.
I wish that you would explain.

I wish that you would find the words.

[thirteen second silence]

I love(*d*) you.
I have always love(*d*) you.

I want(*ed*) to be intimate. I want(*ed*) you to enter
me and make love to me.
But not that.

[eleven second silence]

Not with force.

[eleven second silence]

Not like you did.

[five second silence]

444

You relieved yourself into me. It happened
only once. It didn't happen again. And I don't
understand.

[three second silence]

I don't understand why it happened only once.

*~what did i do wrong?~*
*~why didn't you want me?~*
*~what did i do to make you hate me so very much?~*

---

And yes it did happen. You can't say that it didn't.
There is no other explanation.
There are no other words.

You can't ignore the evidence.
My Davie.

[sound: sobbing]

[voiced: my davie]

[volume: low]

[sound: slow shallow breaths]

You shouldn't ignore Davie.

---

*~do you remember?~*
*~do you still have the visual inside of your mind?~*
*~do you still have the images in front of your eyes?~*
*~do the pictures flicker?~*
*~do the images flash?~*

[sound: a sharp intake of air]

You held me down. I woke to my arms being above my head. I was on my back. Your weight was heavy on me. Your two hands gripped my wrists. Onto the bed. Unable to move. Unable to escape. I wriggled. I squirmed. I tried to move under your weight.

The memory is clear.

[sound: gasping]

[seventeen second silence]

And there was a split of a moment. I am sure that there was a split of a moment when I thought that I was going to enjoy what you were doing.

When I thought that we were going to make love.

That our relationship was going to change.

I've said that before.

[nine second silence]

I am falling falling falling.

[five second silence]

But that split of a moment stopped.
It was cast aside.

It was broken in two.
It was gone when my eyes opened and looked into yours.

[seven second silence]

[sound: sobbing]

Your eyes told me that your intentions were not for us.

[five second silence]

They were for you. Your eyes spoke of anger. Of frustration. Of hatred. Your eyes told me that you had intentions.

I didn't know what to say.
I could have spoken.

But I didn't.

[seven second silence]

*~did that justify what you were doing?~*
*~did that make everything alright?~*

[five second silence]

You see I didn't know what to do.
I felt numb.
My reactions weren't sharp. They weren't quick. I couldn't be quick.
I think that I tried to lift you from me.
In my memory I see my back curving from the bed.

In my memory I try to arch my back and push my stomach up.
With you on top of me.
But I couldn't move your weight. You were too strong. You were too heavy. You were too determined.

[eleven second silence]

I couldn't find the force.

[five second silence]

I didn't want to hurt you. I couldn't hurt you.

[seven second silence]

And I let you hurt me.
I let you use your force and break me.

I love(*d*) you.

---

I remember that you sucked my nipples.

449

*~do you remember?~*

I can still see your mouth around my right nipple.
And then around my left nipple.
I like to think about your mouth around my nipple.
But then you bit my nipples.

*~do you remember?~*
*~was there reason?~*
*~was there purpose?~*

I remember the pain. The pain washes over me. The
memory is red. I feel the pain. I feel your weight.
The grip on my wrists. Your teeth on my nipples.

I remember seeing blood.

[seven second silence]

I know that you preferred my nipples to be covered
in blood.
You sucked. You bit.

[nine second silence]

Pip must have been nearly five years old. She was

asleep in the next room. I thought to scream.
But I didn't.

I don't know if it was to protect you or to protect
your Pip.

*~do you think that i should have?~*
*~did you want me to wake your daughter?~*
*~did you want for your pip to see what you were doing
to me?~*

I could not scream. I have no explanation to offer.
It was not right for me to scream.

I had no right to scream.

I couldn't wake her. I couldn't let Pip come into the
room. Into my bedroom. She loved you. She still
loves you.

I hate(*d*) that she loved you.

[sound: sobbing]

*~did you want pip to see you?~*
*~was she to be the excuse?~*

*~did you want her to hate you?~*
*~would that have made it easier for you to leave?~*
*~would that have justified your desires to go?~*

You wanted to leave us.

*~didn't you?~*

You were looking for a way out.

*~weren't you?~*
*~does sue know that she was your escape ride?~*
*~does she know that you jumped on her back and off you went?~*
*~does sue know how you forced her into the role of frau gothel?~*
*~does sue know that you raped me?~*
*~would you like for me to tell her all that she has missed?~*

[seventeen second silence]

_____

But you know that I'll never tell her.

*~you do realise that don't you?~*

452

[seven second silence]

I'd have told her by now.

[five second silence]

*~is that why you came back?~*
*~did you come back to kill me?~*
*~to silence that act?~*
*~are you erasing your sins?~*
*~is my death your redemption?~*

[seven second silence]

Alex. My Alex.

[three second silence]

I love(*d*) you. I would never harm you. I would
always protect you.
You did not need to kill me.

[five second silence]

---

I didn't understand the rape.

I still don't really understand.

I guess that I never will. Not really.

[eleven second silence]

*~why did you feel that you needed to hurt me?~*
*~why did you feel that you had to force me?~*

[three second silence]

You should have asked. You could have asked.

[five second silence]

I would have let you enter me. I will still let you
enter me.

[eleven second silence]

*~why did you come back to kill me?~*
*~why did you leave me to die?~*

[sound: sobbing]
[sound: slow shallow breaths]

*~why do you hate me alex?~*

[eleven second silence]

---

*~do actions speak louder than words?~*

[voiced: I must sleep]

[volume: low]

[fifteen second silence]

---

I have never spoken those words before. I have never shared that memory.

The redness. The rawness.

The memory of you on me. Of you forcing me. That memory binds us and is part of our history

[seven second silence]

*~are you trying to erase our history?~*
*~why alex why?~*

*~just tell me why?~*
*~please tell me why you hate me so much.~*

[nine second silence]

My words are not enough.

[three second silence]

I cannot express myself. You are not here. You are not listening.
I am waiting for you to emerge from the darkness.

[five second silence]

I am waiting.

[seven second silence]

Waiting.

[nine second silence]

Waiting.

[eleven second silence]

Waiting.

[three second silence]

I am falling.

The images are clear. The memory remains fresh.
Raw. Still seeping blood.

[sound: sobbing]

I will die with that memory.
I need to *blink*. I need to *blink*.

[voiced: blink blink]
[volume: high]

---

I cannot *blink* past that moment.
You used force to enter me. You bruised my
lips. You made my insides raw. I can still feel the
stinging.

[three second silence]

You made me red.

[sound: sobbing]

[sound: breath gasps]

We were not married. We never married. I was not perfect enough for you to marry.

I was not Sue.

[nine second silence]

But I was yours. I am still yours.

[eleven second silence]

I had given you my body. You still own my body. My sexuality is governed by you.

I would never say no to you. I will never say no to you.

But you didn't ask. You didn't use the words.

[five second silence]

You took. You took what you wanted. What you
needed. But my body belonged to you. My body
belongs to you still.

[seven second silence]

It is not the taking that taints the memory. You can
take me. I am yours.
My sexuality is yours.
You are in control.
You have always been in control.

[three second silence]

It is the force. I cannot accept the force.
I cannot accept the violent force.

[three second silence]

There was no need Alex. I would have let you.

[voiced: I love you alex]
[volume: low]

---

I submit myself to you. You are my Lord. You are

my Master.

[seven second silence]

I die for you.

[eleven second silence]

I die and carry your sins with me.

[voiced: I love you alex]

[volume: low]

[voiced: I must sleep]

[volume: low]

---

I crave intimacy.

[seven second silence]

I crave a touch.

[three second silence]

I still hold the wounds.

You have wounded me Alex.

[three second silence]

But soon all will be erased. When I die your pain
dies with me too.

[seven second silence]

There will be no more words Alex.

[five second silence]

*~will that make you care?~*
*~can you hear me alex?~*
*~are you there alex?~*

---

I remember that our life changed during that night.
Our union altered.

[three second silence]

Perhaps it became real.

[seven second silence]

461

Perhaps that was the most honest thing that you ever did.

[five second silence]

Perhaps those actions spoke the truth.

And for all of the confusion that I feel. I gained an honesty that night.

You shattered me. You shattered our bond.

[five second silence]

But you were being honest.

[five second silence]

*~that's right isn't it?~*

From that day, I knew that you would not protect me. I realised that you would never have protected me and that you never would protect me.
I knew that I could not trust you. I knew that I had been wrong to ever trust you.

462

But I still love(*d*) you.

I even think that I love(*d*) you more.

[five second silence]

And your coming back here again tonight.

*~you are being honest again aren't you?~*

I understand that now.

[five second silence]

I understand why you have killed me.
I think that I love you even more.

[five second silence]

I am falling Alex.
I am falling.

I feel so very nauseous. I must not vomit. I must not

463

vomit. I feel so tired.

[eleven second silence]

I must not sleep.

I must not sleep.

I must not sleep.

[sound: a guttural laugh]
[sound: breath gasps]
[seven second silence]

_____

I remember that the days afterwards you were quiet.
You were not cruel. Your mood was low.
I remember thinking that your frustrations had been
removed.

[seventeen second silence]

I remember thinking that our life was altering.
I remember thinking that we were going to start
again.

[seven second silence]

You never said that to me.

*~don't be angry with me alex!~*
*~please don't be angry!~*

I misread. I read incorrectly.
I coloured in the holes. I think that I coloured in
those holes.

[eleven second silence]

---

The forcing happened only once. The you entering
me in the night happened only once.

Just once.

But I have spent the rest of my days waiting for you
to enter me again.

[seven second silence]

You hurt me Alex. But with that physical hurting
you made me feel alive again.

I had something real to consider. The pain was
physical. It wasn't a state of mind.
I could breathe again.

[three second silence]

But I hurt myself even more.

After that night I would sleep on my back. I would
sleep naked. On my back. With my legs open.
I was welcoming you into me.
But you didn't.

*~did you know alex?~*

[five second silence]

And I know that every night that you didn't scratch
into me.
It hurt me even more.
I was confused. I didn't understand.

[sound: wardrobe door opening]

---

And there were consequences.

*~do i need to explain the consequences to you?~*

I am giving a label. I am speaking the words.

[voiced: I'm pregnant]

[volume: low]

[voiced: I'm pregnant]

[volume: low]

[sound: slow shallow breaths]


[seventeen second silence]

This is where it all goes wrong. This is where it all gets worse.

[five second silence]

The consequences of your actions. The consequence of force.

A consequence.

*~how can i call him a consequence?~*

[sound: sobbing]

[voiced: my davie]

[volume: low]

[sound: slow shallow breaths]

There is a living memory. There is a breathing consequence.

Davie.

My beautiful son Davie.

[sound: sobbing]

[five second silence]

With that entering.
With that force.
You left inside me the sperm that was to become our Davie.
There was never any talk of abortion. The word was not mentioned.

[fifteen second silence]

_____

Just over eight months later.

[five second silence]

Your son was born.

Out of force. Into a fragmented family.

[seventeen second silence]

His presence was a reminder.

[nine second silence]

His body spoke the words that your actions had
produced.

[five second silence]

He was created from anger. From hatred. From force.

[voiced: my davie]
[volume: low]
[sound: breath gasps]
[sound: sobbing]

―――――――――――――――――――――――――――――]

And you hate(*d*) him.
And I love(*d*) him.

[five second silence]

He tied us tighter together.

[seven second silence]

My Davie. Our Davie. Never your Davie.

[voiced: my davie]

[volume: low]

[sound: sobbing]

[sound: breath gasps]

[five second silence]

---

But then it all fell apart didn't it?

[voiced: I must sleep]

[volume: low]

[five second silence]

You couldn't be a part of our family any longer.

[eleven second silence]

And you found Sue.

[five second silence]

And Sue became pregnant.

*~did you force her too?~*

[five second silence]

I am falling. I must not vomit. I must not vomit.

[nineteen second silence]

And then you decided that Sue was the woman whom you would marry. That she would become your wife.

[nineteen second silence]

I must not sleep. I must not sleep.

[eleven minute silence]

---

And then tonight.
I heard a familiar voice.

[eleven second silence]

I heard your tones. You told the children, **leave**. You told the children, **get into my car**.

[five second silence]

I heard you.

[five second silence]

I heard your heavy footsteps. I knew that you had come back to me.

[eleven second silence]

You entered my room and I threw my arms around you. I could not stop the tears from falling.

[five second silence]

But you did not want my arms. You pushed me away from you.

[eleven second silence]

*~why did you push me away alex?~*
*~why did you look at me with disgust?~*

[eleven second silence]

This isn't how the story is supposed to unfold. This isn't how the story was supposed to end.

[three second silence]

You came back to me.
You brought me my box of painkillers. You brought me my box of sleeping tablets.
You brought me a glass of water.
You brought me scissors and a comb.

[seventeen second silence]

You told me, **you should cut your hair**.

[five second silence]

You made everything clear to me in the giving of gifts.

[nine second silence]

I love(*d*) you.

[eleven second silence]

You know that I will do anything for you.

[five second silence]

I know that you will lead me into your kingdom and I will live the rest of my life in joy and love.

[nine second silence]

You have shown me the way towards a true happily ever after.

[eleven second silence]
[sound: slow shallow breaths]

You left me. I am waiting for you to return.

[eleven second silence]

I knew what I had to do. You did not use words.

[five second silence]

I took the painkillers. I took my sleeping tablets. I
took them all.
I cut my hair.

I am waiting.
I am falling.
*Blink blink.*

[eleven second silence]

_____

My room is a box. A black box. A sometimes ruby
red box. You are leading me out of this box and
into your kingdom.

[sound: breath gasps]

[five second silence]

The view from my window is ever changing. I
see the sand. I see the sea. And that image is my
painting mounted in a chipped red window frame. A
sometimes black window frame. A perfect square.

A perfect painting. A painting that holds a memory

of you and me.

[sound: breath gasps]

[seven second silence]

I love you.

I worship you.
I will only serve you.

[sound: breath gasps]

[five second silence]

*Blink. Blink.*

[sound: breath gasps]

[sound: slow shallow breaths]

[voiced: I must sleep]

[volume: low]

*~will you please stay with me until my eyes close?~*

I will not *blink* again.

[eleven minute silence]

# Black Boxes

[voiced: pip]

[volume: low]

# BLACK
# BOXES

## After the crash

# Obituary

## Lewis, Anabel

Born March 1969
Died March 2006

**Lewis,** Anabel (Ana) *was called home by our heavenly father.* Passed away in hospital, Sunday 26 March 2006. Aged 37 years, beloved mother of Pippa and David Edwards. Funeral service to take place at St Paul's Church, Mortney at 2:30 p.m., Wednesday 29 March 2006. Followed by burial in Mortney Cemetery. The family requests no flowers. The family requests no children attend the funeral or burial. For all enquiries please contact T. A. Davison, Funeral Director on 0151 356 5677

# Selling

---

**From:** Premier Gold [mailto:sam@premiergold.
co.uk]
**Sent**: Wed 05/04/2006 09:32
**To:** Alexander Edwards
**Cc:** Penny Edwards-Knight
**Subject:** Re: The sale of your property

Dear Mr Edwards,
Just a quick update to keep you informed.
Your property details have been released in a
customer match mailout this morning. I have
attached the details to this email for your
records.
If you have any queries, do not hesitate to email
or call.

Sam Gallagher
Director.

**Attachments:**
17SeaViewdetails_AE07-06-06.doc

# PREMIER GOLD

*Independent Estate Agents*

## 17, Sea View Avenue, Monkseaton

Offers in the region of £325,000

## FEATURES

- Detached house
- Three bedrooms
- Master en suite
- Two reception rooms
- Conservatory
- Gas C H & double glazing
- Driveway & double garage
- Gardens front & rear

Premier Gold are pleased to offer into the market this superbly presented detached house, situated on this favoured residential development close to local amenities and convenient for access to town centre. Extended by the present owners, the property benefits from gas central heating, double glazing, an alarm and includes entrance lobby, downstairs WC, hallway, living room, dining room, conservatory, breakfasting kitchen, master bedroom with en suite, two further bedrooms and family bathroom/WC. The property hosts driveway parking, a double garage and there are pleasant gardens to front and rear.

Early viewing is strongly recommended.

# Buying

---

**From:** Clive Perkin Estates [mailto:cperkin@ cliveperkinestates.co.uk]
**Sent:** Thursday 11/05/2006 11:35
**To:** Alexander Edwards
**Cc:** Penny Edwards-Knight
**Subject:** Re: Anchoring

Alex,
Hope all is well with you and yours.
Your mother has asked me to email the details of 'Anchoring' to you. It is a quite outstanding property that would be ideal for your family's needs.
I look forward to arranging a viewing,
Clive.

Clive Perkin
Director.


**Attachments:**
Anchoringdetails_AE06-07-06.doc

## cp Est. *Clive Perkin Estates*

# 'Anchoring',

### Mortney, Cheshire

# £735,000

**The property has undergone a
widespread scheme of restoration and
extension to create a quite exceptional
property which offers light and
spacious accommodation.**

The property occupies a plot extending over five
acres and enjoys magnificent ground and first floor
rural views. We recommend a full interior inspection
to appreciate the numerous striking features
on offer and the deceivingly spacious and light
accommodation.

Situated within the picturesque village of Mortney,
the property is convenient for a range of amenities.

The accommodation comprises:
VESTIBULE.
SPACIOUS RECEPTION HALL.
DINING ROOM.
LOUNGE.
FAMILY ROOM KITCHEN/BREAKFAST ROOM.
UTILITY ROOM.
LIBRARY.
DOWNSTAIRS WC.
FIVE BEDROOMS ALL WITH EN SUITE SHOWER
STUDY.
BATHROOM.
OUTSIDE DOUBLE GARAGE.
LARGE WORKSHOP.
LAWNED GARDEN TO THE FRONT WITH WELL
STOCKED BEDS AND BORDERS.
A PATIO AREA TO THE REAR.
INDOOR SWIMMING POOL.

Viewing is strictly by appointment only.
Telephone: Clive Perkin Estates – 0151 3763357

# Black Boxes

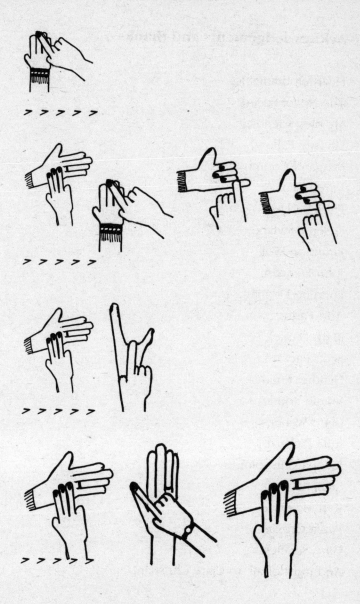

489

## Acknowledgements and thanks

Heartfelt thanks to:
The Novel Racers,
My blog friends,
Lindsey Fallow,
Margaret Coombs,
Karen Clark,
Patrick Clark,
Helen Rowland,
Jamieson Wolf,
John Dennan,
Lorraine Dennan,
Ario Farin,
Mark Daniel,
Scott Pack,
Heather Smith,
Jennie Routley,
Clare Weber,
Julie Pickard,
Joanna Chisholm,
Richard Wells,
Karl McIntyre,
Paula Groves,
Gary Smailes.
And most of all, to Clare Christian.

# 1980

On March 26 1980, I was six years, four months and two days old. I was dressed and ready for school. It was 8:06am on my digital watch. My mother was still in bed. I went into her room to wake her. I found her lying on top of her duvet cover. She wasn't wearing any clothes. Her ocean eyes were open. She wasn't sleeping. And from the corner of her mouth, a line

of
**lumpy**
**sick**

joined her to the pool that was stuck to her cheek. Next to her, on her duvet I saw an empty bottle. Vodka. And there were eleven tablets. Small round and white. And I saw a scrap of ripped paper. There were words on it.

*jude, i have gone in search of adam.*
*i love you baby.*

I didn't understand. But I took the note. It was mine. I shoved it into the pocket of my grey school skirt. I crumpled it in. Then. Then I climbed next to her. I spooned into her. Moulded into a question mark. Her stale sick mingled and lumped into my shiny hair. I stayed with my mother, until the warmth from her body transferred into me. We were not disturbed until my father returned from work At 6:12pm.

£7.99 PB
ISBN-13: 978-1-906321-02-4

"There is little in the way of relief in this harrowing first novel, but Smailes' sensitivity towards her subjects – and the poetry of her writing – carry the story."
*Financial Times*

"A unique, exciting and unforgettable read."
Ray Robinson, author of *Electricity*

"Staccato prose that crackles with experience"
Danny Rhodes, author of *Asboville*

"An engrossing and touching read from a new talent."
*The Big Issue in the North*